Between CONTROL AND CHAOS

WILLOW FOX

Published by Slow Burn Publishing

Cover Design by GetCovers

Edited by Marla VanHoy

Proofread by Ami K., and Jen S.

ONE

LUCA

"What do you mean *my wife* is missing? Is Zeke all right?" I rush past my father in haste, hurrying to the playroom to find Zeke standing and coloring at the easel.

"As you can see, Zeke is fine," my father says, his expression grim.

How long has he known Harper has been missing? Why didn't anyone call me the moment her disappearance was noticed?

I'm choking back silent sobs, my heart in my throat with worry. I hurry out of the playroom, not wanting Zeke to overhear and start crying.

He's been doing so well, finally sleeping in his bed again and mostly sleeping through the night. We have Nikki and Paige to thank for helping get him back into his routine after the nightmares.

Nightmares caused by Santino DeLuca.

I blame my father, Dante, for those hellish dreams. Had he protected my family as promised, Zeke would be blissfully unaware of the dangers of the world. And Harper, she'd be home safe.

"Where is Harper? What do you mean she's missing?" I rattle off one question after another. "She's supposed to be at work."

Clearly, she made it here to drop off Zeke. Did she not make it work? "Did anyone find her car?" I grab my keys from my pocket, prepared to drive the path to the bar to see if she broke down.

It'd dark outside; perhaps she followed the road or foolishly took a shortcut and got lost in the woods. The bar isn't that far from the compound.

"Something happened at the bar," Dante says and glances at Moreno, who is walking down the hallway, approaching us. "We're not quite sure what. She was bartending and then—she was gone."

"Gone?" I repeat. Harper wouldn't just disappear. Not while at work. "What about her phone?"

"Still at the bar," my father says.

"Her car?" I glance from my father to Moreno.

"Also at the bar. I don't believe she left willingly."

"Of course not!" She wouldn't leave Zeke. I'd like to think she wouldn't leave me, either, but I know for a fact that she'd never abandon her son.

"We're going over surveillance, but there isn't much to go on. There's no surveillance inside the bar, for obvious reasons, and the camera outside doesn't show much. The window from when she was last seen until someone noticed she was missing is rather wide. There are several vehicles leaving during that time frame."

Are they telling me they have nothing? "No leads?"

"We have a few ideas," Moreno says and glances at Dante, "but they are more like theories with potential for who might have taken Harper."

"So, we're in agreement she didn't run away. Good." I fold my arms across my chest. Not that I believe Harper would have fled again. "What about the

DeLucas?" I ask. It seems the most plausible explanation. They are the obvious enemies.

"I have someone on the inside. If it's the DeLucas, we'll know soon."

"Are you sure you can trust your source? Weren't you concerned he betrayed you?" I ask, remembering when Harper confronted Dante, just a few short weeks ago in his office. After Santino's death.

"She and I have no reason to believe in her betrayal. It is more likely she was unaware until it was too late. We still have good intel coming in from her."

"Who is your source?" If Dante trusts me, he should give me that information.

Dante shakes his head. "No one you should know. The fact I've told you it's a woman is dangerous enough for her. If she has information, she'll provide it to us shortly."

"How soon?" Does he not realize the urgency in finding Harper? The longer she's gone, the less chance we'll have of recovering her alive.

I click my tongue and grimace. "What about—there was this guy at the bar, he ordered drinks for himself and for Harper. What if it's him?" Something felt off about that night, at least to me.

Dante's eyes tighten. "When was this?"

Moreno silently exchanges a look with Dante that makes my stomach roil. Bile rises to my throat, and I swallow the burn back down.

It takes me only a second to recall the information. "Last Saturday. Can you comb through receipts?"

"I'll look into it. I might have to drive over to the bar —" Moreno says.

"Why was your wife drinking on the job?" Dante's question comes out more like an accusation. "Was it a slap in the face for making her work for me?"

I scoff at his suggestion and back away from him. "Not everything is about you, *father*." The words come off snide and with disdain.

He's certainly not my favorite person, and he's not even making my top five.

"We will find Harper; after all, she's family. We don't leave our own behind."

I can't help but flinch at the realization that he now considers her family.

Mafia.

"Do whatever is necessary to find her," Dante says and waves his hand, dismissing Moreno to go and work.

"Wait! She told me his name." I pinch the bridge of my nose, my eyes slam shut, trying to remember what she'd said. "It starts with a J—"

Jeremy.

John.

Jacob.

"Jayden!" My eyes flash open as I meet my father's stare.

He flinches and grimaces.

"Does that name mean anything to you?" I ask, but already, there's a hint of recognition and anger, his hands balling into fists.

"Fucking Jaxson Monroe," Dante growls and storms toward his office.

Who is that?

The name means nothing to me.

"What's next? I can't just sit around and wait for a ransom demand." My breath catches in my throat, my world spins wildly on its axis, out of control.

Dante opens the office door. The room feels suffocating, and I back up a step. "Are we sure the police didn't show up? Maybe she was arrested?" For some reason, that would be the easier solution, the happier ending, which doesn't seem happy to me. But I could hire her a lawyer, and at least I'd know she's safe. Alive.

"Jayden is behind this mess. I can feel it." Dante glances at Moreno. "Go find him. I don't care if you have to wake *all of them* and interrogate them, find my daughter-in-law."

He gestures for me to step into his office, and I relent, trudging inside. I can't sit. I'm filled with nervous energy, and I stand behind the office chair, my hands on the back of the chair while Dante comes around to sit behind the desk.

"What would Jayden want with Harper?" I ask,

completely unaware of who he is and why he would go after my wife.

Dante huffs under his breath, the answer to him, simple. "To get to me."

"Harper wouldn't betray you," I say, confident that after what happened with Santino, she'd have zero desire to spill any of the family's secrets or turn on Dante. She's too heavily involved now after killing Santino; it would only incriminate both of us.

His jaw is tight and his eyes flicker. "She's not stupid enough to rat you and herself out, but she might betray *me*."

"She wouldn't," I say, instantly defending my wife. "Harper knows to keep her mouth shut because all of it ties back to us. She's learned her lesson, understands her place in the business."

Dante stares at me, raising an eyebrow, seemingly unconvinced. "Does she? Harper hasn't been working for me for very long. I've had men with more years under their belt betray me."

"She's not like any of your men," I roar.

Harper is different.

She's softer.

Kinder.

Warmer.

She doesn't deserve this.

"Are we sure Jayden is responsible for her abduction? We need to rule out all possibilities," I say. While I appreciate Moreno taking a car to check out Jayden or whoever he thinks is involved in Harper's disappearance, time is of the essence. Letting any other potential leads slip through the cracks could be deadly.

"Who else do you think might have taken her?" Dante asks, getting right to the point. "Jayden is our best suspect."

"Do you have any other enemies?" I ask, staring at my father, assuming he's the reason that she's been taken.

His eyes flicker, and he clasps his hands together on the desk. Slowly, he tilts his head, his gaze never leaving mine. "Who's to say I'm the one responsible or to blame? Your wife has a way of making enemies, son."

I scoff and shake my head, pushing myself away from the chair and stalking the length of his office. It's not very large, considering the size of the compound. But I suppose since it's an interior room, it wasn't intended to be large, it was more about protection, safety, and security.

"Aside from the DeLucas, who I blame, you are responsible for the mess we've dealt with. What other enemies does my wife have?" I approach Dante from the other side of my chair, standing over his desk, awaiting a response.

He merely shrugs. "Her parents don't seem fond of her."

"They didn't kidnap Harper." I roll my eyes at his suggestion.

"Never said they did. You asked about enemies. I suspect she may have a few others growing up. She's got a baby daddy, Luca."

"Who wanted nothing to do with Zeke." I grind my teeth together, nearly chipping them, and shake my head.

"Perhaps that's changed. We should look into this fellow, whoever he is, make sure that he isn't after

Harper and Zeke." Dante rises from his chair and stalks around to the filing cabinet. "I'll reach out to my police contact and make sure there's no involvement from the baby daddy."

Nova storms into Dante's office without so much as knocking. "Where's Harper?" The worry in her eyes tells me that she's heard her best friend, *my wife*, is missing.

She's not asking me.

Her question is directed at my father.

"We don't know." He's calm, collected, like he's done all this before and he's not the least bit concerned about the outcome.

This isn't just one of his men who disappeared.

She's my fucking wife.

"How'd you hear?" I ask, glancing at Nova.

"Ashton heard Moreno and Nico were heading out. He offered to go with them, but Moreno suggested he could do more here to find Harper." Nova stares at me, her eyes glassy. "Who would take her?"

"I'm not sure," I say. "It could be this guy, Jayden, from the bar. Do you remember her telling you anything about him?"

Nova's brow pinches. "She doesn't talk about work." She glances from Dante back to me. "Someone at the bar? You have all those cameras installed—"

"Outside the premises. Yes, but inside, there aren't cameras because it's where we do business. We're not recording inside for problematic individuals to get ahold of."

He means the police or feds.

"You forced my wife to work in *your* bar, and you don't have any idea what happened when she disappeared on *your* watch." My jaw ticks as I stand toe-to-toe with Dante. "Fix this!" I demand.

His eyes flinch for a fraction of a second. To almost anyone else, it would be unnoticeable. "We wait," Dante says, his voice calm.

"For what?" I glare at him. "A ransom call? Should I just stare at my phone, hoping someone will reach out demanding money?"

Nova clears her throat, interrupting the storm between Dante and me. “What about the DeLucas? They broke into our home, we killed one of them, maybe they want revenge?”

Dante purses his lips. “It’s possible they’re behind the abduction, but if they are, as I’ve told Luca, we will find out soon enough.”

“How? From a ransom call? What if they don’t want anything except to hurt her?”

I wince, the realization a painful possibility I don’t want to acknowledge.

“We have someone on the inside,” Dante says. “If she’s alive and being held captive by the DeLucas, we will know soon enough.”

I don’t even want to consider that as a possibility. After Massimo’s and Santino’s deaths, if they have Harper, it’s not going to be for ransom.

It’ll be revenge.

Nova’s voice is soft, hesitant, as she says, “Maybe Harper will escape and call you.”

It’s wishful thinking.

Not that I don't think Harper wouldn't try to flee, but whoever has her, they're not going to just let her go that easily. I shove Dante out of the way and take the seat behind his desk, taking command.

"What the hell are you doing?" Dante's tone is fueled with shock, but he's not screaming at me to move. Even if he were, I'd ignore him.

I open his desk drawer, retrieve a notepad and pen and scribble down every possibility as a list.

Man in bar offering Harper drinks. Jayden?

DeLuca's men. Who is in charge?

Zeke's bio dad.

It's currently a short list. I glance at Nova. "Anyone else?"

"What if it's someone like the feds? I mean the police would be loud, noticeable, if they came to arrest her. But what if it were someone who wanted her to turn against the family?" Nova suggests.

I grind my teeth together, praying that it isn't the feds who got to Harper.

Feds?

Hospital.

"Do you think she'd have walked to the hospital, Luca?" Nova glances at me skeptically as she studies my list.

"No, but if she did escape, she doesn't have her I.D. on her or her phone, maybe she hit her head," I suggest. Right now, I'm hoping for a case of amnesia over a kidnapping. I feel physically sick.

Dante clears his throat. "I'll have my men check the hospital, call to see if anyone matching her description was brought in tonight."

"Any other ideas?" I ask, glancing at Nova and Dante.

Dante examines the notepad and taps his finger on the second line about DeLuca's men. "Livia DeLuca, Santino's widow, is running his empire. She's as cruel and cutthroat as her father-in-law Massimo, from what I hear. She already murdered two capos who dared to consider taking her throne."

"Livia, it is," I say, putting her name down on my list beside DeLuca's men. "She would certainly have a grudge against Harper, for killing Santino."

Nova huffs under her breath. "He broke into Zeke's room. Tried to kidnap a child. Sounds like a monster to me. And one with a motive."

I meet Nova's stare. "Are you in?"

I know she despises what we do. Deep down, she thinks she's better than us, smarter because she isn't tied up in our sinister dealings.

A small part of me is glad she's protected, naïve.

She rolls her lips together. There's trepidation behind her features. "The bar guy, Jayden, seems like a long shot. I'd bet anything it's Livia, the widow, behind Harper's abduction."

I bite down on my tongue.

I can't know without a doubt, not yet. There isn't any evidence, nothing to go on, and we can't exactly reach out to the police.

"We take two teams and work out both leads. We can't waste any time," I say.

Dante watches me with enthusiasm, clearly pleased I'm taking the lead on my missing wife.

“Ashton is here already, but I’ll bring in Sophia and Liam. At the very least, they can help run down leads,” Dante says.

“Are there any of Luca’s friends you don’t intend to hire?” Nova snaps at my father.

“I would think you’d be happy for the extra bodies to scout the woods, make sure that Harper didn’t just get lost in the dark.”

I’d love to claim denial, but there’s no way Harper got turned around and couldn’t find the building. I don’t buy it. “That’s more than just a little highly unlikely. It’s impractical. Even if the light outside was out, there is enough light out front that she could have found her way to the parking lot and inside through the main doors. Someone took her.”

Dante sighs. “I agree as well, that seems the most likely scenario. The question is who.”

TWO

HARPER

Kicking and screaming did absolutely nothing and with the duct tape secured across my mouth, a black bag over my head, I have no idea where I am.

Time doesn't feel as though it passes; it stretches on forever and stalls, like Father Time is a cruel trickster playing a joke.

It's complete and utter darkness. The vehicle hums and roars, twisting through mountainous roads and then slows to a crawl.

Has it been minutes or hours?

Are we there?

The engine doesn't shut off. We stall.

Are we stuck in traffic or waiting for something? I don't hear the engine of a train, but we could be back several car lengths if we're stuck waiting for one to pass.

The vehicle roars again, the driver heavy on the gas as I'm thrown around the backseat.

Time seems to stretch and expand, snap and bend.

My heart pounds wildly in my chest as I listen to the sounds; it feels like we're on gravel and we finally pull to an abrupt halt.

The doors open and close and then I feel myself being dragged out of the vehicle and escorted up several steps.

I can't speak. Can't scream.

Fighting is useless with my arms secured behind my back, my vision blind, my mouth silenced.

Steps up.

Five.

Then hard flooring.

No plush carpet under my feet.

I try to take in every detail.

"Watch your step." It's the same male voice, the one I heard who abducted me.

The man from the bar.

Jayden.

What does he want with me? Does he work for Santino DeLuca or Dante?

He drags me down several stairs. Fourteen, to be exact, and then removes the bag from my head.

A single bulb illuminates the darkened cellar.

"Don't scream," he warns and removes the tape from my mouth.

I reach out to bite him, and he smacks me across the face.

Wincing, the burn stings, and he shoves me into a metal folding chair, my arms still bound behind my back.

"I was really hoping we didn't have to do this the hard way, Harper."

"Who do you work for?" I stare up at him, hatred in my eyes as I try to take in my surroundings. There's one exit door, two egress windows. The windows aren't the most easily accessible, but I could probably slide out of them if he leaves me alone. I'd just have to climb to reach them.

Already, I'm plotting my escape.

Jayden laughs and smiles down at me, not the least bit tense. "I don't work for anyone. I'm here to help you."

I snort at his offer of help. "You could start by taking off the restraints."

He retrieves a pocketknife and gestures for me to turn around. Within seconds, he unbinds my hands. I pull them forward around myself and rub at my wrists, the pain searing from being too tight.

"I apologize for the theatrics, but we had to make it look like you were kidnapped."

I huff and fold my arms across my chest. "You did kidnap me!" I shout at him, loud enough that if we're not alone, someone else will hear me.

"I borrowed you," Jayden says and smiles. "Harper McKenna."

"It's Harper Ricci," I correct him. I'm not sure why I do; maybe I should have pretended that I wasn't married. It's not like I wear my wedding band at the bar. The tips are better when I leave it off.

A sly smile spreads across Jayden's face. "I know. We did a background check on you, thoroughly vetted every detail of your life. You're married to Luca Ricci. You also have a son, Zeke."

I inhale sharply as I stare up at Jayden. It's just the two of us. Perhaps I can convince him to let me go or overpower him.

"If you so much as lay a finger on my husband or my son—"

"Relax," Jayden is all smiles, which only infuriates me further, "I'm here to offer you help. You wanted out of the mafia, away from your father-in-law, Dante, is that correct?"

I stare at him, perplexed.

How could he know that?

At least, I had wanted help months ago. Even weeks ago, I'd have been happy to turn on Dante, but not now. Not after what happened with Santino.

I'd be putting Luca and myself in danger.

"I don't know what you're talking about. Mafia?" I ask, giving him a look of disbelief as I play dumb. "You're the monster from what I can tell, abducting a woman from her job. You really should let me go before you spend the rest of your miserable life behind bars."

Jayden runs a hand through his short-cropped dark hair. His eyes blend into the darkness of the basement he's keeping me in. "Come on, you work for Dante Ricci. You're his daughter-in-law. You have to know he's mafia."

"You're mafia," I retort, like a teenager shooting insults. I refuse to acknowledge Dante is mafia, because it would be incriminating myself.

His eyes wince and I see the worry lines appear on his forehead.

Did he really think I'd flip on Dante after *he* abducted me?

"You met Jaxson's daughter; you were at the police station—"

I hold his stare, unwilling to so much as flinch. "You're mistaken. You kidnapped the wrong girl."

His face reddens, and I can't tell if it's anger or irritation. Either way, he's pissed. He curses under his breath. "This is not how I saw this going," Jayden mutters under his breath.

"Yeah, this isn't how I saw my shift going, either. Take me back to the bar before anyone notices I'm missing."

I forgot to wear my watch today and my damn phone is still at the bar. There's no clock and it's dark outside, giving zero indication of the hour.

Jayden retrieves his phone from his pocket and scratches the back of his neck. He looks nervous and flustered. "Yeah, it's a bit late for that."

Relief floods through me. If Dante knows I'm missing, then he'll come for me. His men won't let Jayden keep me locked up in his basement forever.

He sighs and grabs a chair, sitting across from me. "Listen, I thought I was doing you a favor, trying to help you get out of the family. I saw you were a new employee for Dante, when I asked around and realized who you were—I was just trying to help."

"You have a funny way of helping. Let me go. We can all put this behind us."

"Can we?" Jayden asks, glancing me over. "I don't want any trouble with Dante."

His phone buzzes in his hand, and I glance at the screen as the name *Jaxson Monroe* is calling.

"My boss," he says, pressing his lips together. He silences the call. "We don't have much time. I swear on my life, I thought I was doing the right thing, Harper."

"Abducting me? Are you insane?"

He laughs and hangs his head. "Maybe I am. My niece was taken when she was younger. I guess I just want to be the hero."

"Heroes don't kidnap people!" I shout at him.

Jayden scoots back, the chair scraping against the concrete floor. "You're right. But if I let you go, and you go back to your father-in-law and tell him I'm involved, it's going to get messy."

"You're worried he'll kill you." I pin him with my stare.

Jayden merely nods. "I was trying to do good. Not that Dante would see it that way. I don't have any issue with him."

Could have fooled me.

"Everyone knows Dante is mafia. If you don't know that, well, you're kidding yourself or they're good at hiding it," Jayden says. He stares at me, his eyes two dark pools luring me in. "I've heard chatter, I know my boss has been involved in some shady shit recently, helping Dante. It's all—a bit strange." He seems to be talking to himself more than to me. Like he's trying to figure out what the hell is going on.

Makes two of us.

Dante keeps me out of a lot of his shit.

"You ever hear about Dante trafficking women and children?" Jayden asks and stands.

My shoulders straighten as I shake my head. "He wouldn't do that." I don't deceive him or myself, pretending Dante is a good man, but DeLuca is the monster and Jayden, I'm not sure. Maybe he's trying to help, or maybe he's working for DeLuca in secret. I can't help but worry that Jayden is pressing me for information for some other reason.

But the concern laced on his face is genuine.

"Someone has been trafficking them through town. My boss helped reunite the girls with their families, the ones who had disappeared. But some of those girls, sending them home would have been a death sentence or worse..." his voice trails off.

"Maybe your boss is the bad guy."

Jayden paces the length of the cellar. "No, Jaxson is straight as an arrow when it comes to right and wrong. There is no morally gray with him."

"Yet he was involved with the trafficking operation," I point out what Jayden just told me.

He shakes his head in utter denial. "Absolutely not!" He stops pacing and glares at me, stepping closer, into my personal space. Jayden leans down, meeting my stare. He's fueled by anger and coldness that scares me. "Jaxson is a saint compared to these men."

"These men who don't have a name," I point out.

"It has to be Dante." Jayden pushes off his heels and paces the room again.

I glance behind myself briefly, toward the door, my only escape with Jayden blocking the egress windows, not that I could easily climb out with him in the room.

"Dante wouldn't kidnap..."

I press my lips together, knowing full well that he did abduct a child. But an entire human trafficking ring. Absolutely not.

He had kidnapped that child to stop that type of behavior from a man who was involved in hurting children. I rub my forehead, knowing full-well that DeLuca is the man or the mafia family that Jayden should be after.

But do I tell him?

Jayden's phone rings again, and he silences it again, ignoring the caller.

"Aren't you going to answer that? It seems kind of important if he keeps calling you," I say, keeping my voice soft, feminine, unsuspecting.

Jayden sighs and heads for the stairs, retrieving his phone from his pocket.

"Hello?" he says, halfway up the stairs.

"Help! Jayden's kidnapped me! I'm in a dark basement!" I scream at the top of my lungs, praying that Jaxson, the man on the other end of the phone, will hear me and come help.

THREE

JAXSON

I've been trying for the past twenty-minutes to get through to Jayden. He's not answering his phone, and I know he's avoiding my calls because they keep getting sent to voicemail after a couple of rings.

What the hell is he up to?

"Hello?" Jayden finally answers, and he sounds a bit out of breath.

"What the hell took you so long?" I grumble at him, and in the background, I hear a faint female voice screaming. It's mumbled and muffled. "What the fuck is going on, Jayden?"

He clears his throat. "Just the television," he answers. "Sorry, I muted it."

I don't hear anything suspicious, and I pause, listening again, but just his breathing. "Dante called me, wants to know why you were hanging out at the Bloody Rogue."

"I can't go to the bar after work for a drink?" Jayden asks.

Everyone in town, at least our crew, we all know the Bloody Rogue is owned by Dante Ricci. The same Dante Ricci who runs the Italian mafia. Typically, we steer clear of their venues as much as we can.

"What's really going on?"

"Is that my dad?" Izzie's voice pipes up from the other side.

My stomach flops. "Why is my daughter hanging out with you?" Izzie is in her mid-twenties, there's no reason for her to spend time with Jayden.

"She was helping me with a project," Jayden says, clearing his throat.

"Does that project have anything to do with a

missing young woman, Harper Ricci? Let me talk to my daughter."

I hear the phone being passed down to my daughter. "Hi, Dad."

"Please tell me you're not involved in Harper Ricci's disappearance."

"I'm not involved in Harper Ricci's disappearance," she repeats a little too quickly. My daughter has never been good at lying to me. One of the advantages of what I do for a living, I'm able to read people.

"Where is she, Izzie?"

"Umm, in the basement."

Jayden's voice echoes from the other side, slightly distant but still rather loud. "Fuck! Why did you have to tell him? He's going to fucking turn us into the cops!"

"I-I didn't know what Uncle Jayden had planned," Izzie stammers, and I believe my daughter. "He told me we were helping a young woman escape the mafia."

Izzie wouldn't get involved in a kidnapping, not intentionally. She's smarter than that fool. Why the hell had I hired him again?

Oh, right, because he was useful when working undercover and helping with missions. Well, right now, I was second guessing every decision I'd ever made regarding Jayden Scott.

"Where is the girl now?" I ask, grimacing, realizing she's nearly my daughter's age. If someone took Izzie, I'd go to the ends of the earth to find her and bring her home.

"She's downstairs in the basement. She's already seen Jayden's face; she knows him, but I wore a mask."

"Good. Don't let her be able to identify you. I don't need you getting thrown behind bars for your Uncle Jayden's foolish actions."

Jayden married my sister, Skylar, making him Izzie's uncle. A shitty one at that, but he showed up, came around, tried to be part of the family, and with time, I reluctantly gave him a job.

Biggest mistake of my life.

Had I known he'd get Izzie involved in this nonsense, I'd have let the wolves have him. After all, that's where he belonged.

And it isn't like Jayden and I had met solely through Skylar. We'd served time together overseas; we were in the same unit, brothers. Even in the military, trouble seemed to follow him.

"I want you to go home, stay out of trouble. Now, give the phone back to your uncle."

"Yes, Dad." Izzie doesn't so much as question my authority. She recognizes when she's in danger, and I'm trying to protect her.

The phone changes hands and Jayden clears his throat. "Yeah?"

"You need to let Harper go."

"I can't do that. She knows who I am, she'll go straight to the cops."

"Then convince her to tell the Riccis that someone else was behind the abduction. I'm sure there are other enemies out there, use them. What were you planning on doing?"

"I hadn't been planning on it taking that long to get her here. There was an accident that shut down the bypass road. I had expected her to be gone less than an hour, back at the bar, and hoped no one would notice. They'd figure she took her break, and we'd have intel on Dante. She'd be working for us."

"I didn't ask you to go after Dante, and good job fucking that up," I growl at him.

Why does he have to work for me? Had I left him doing his own thing, maybe then my daughter wouldn't have gotten involved.

He still would have met Skylar, though, because it wasn't like I had anything to do with that introduction.

I wanted the two of them kept far apart.

And then he went and married my sister.

"I'll figure it out," Jayden grumbles under his breath.

"You harm a hair on her head," I threaten, "and so help me, Jayden, you're a dead man."

FOUR

HARPER

The moment Jayden is upstairs on the phone, he slams the door shut, silencing my screams for help. I hurry out of the metal folding chair, grab it and carry it toward the egress window, using the chair to stand.

There aren't any locks or security systems with an alarm blaring when I manage to open the window.

I climb out into the darkness.

I'm underdressed for the night air and shiver. It's nearly pitch black and there's only a sliver of moon in the sky. Not enough to offer light to find my way to the main road.

From the looks of it, I'm at a cabin, someplace in the woods.

Great.

That describes too many remote locations. I can't even fathom what town I'm in right now.

I don't have my phone, no car. I sneak away from the property, quiet as I hurry down the gravel road and follow it down the mountain.

My hands are freezing, and I wrap them around myself to keep warm. The short-sleeved shirt with a dip in my cleavage is not practical for outside. But I wasn't expecting to be stuck out in the cold.

I was dressed for the bar, attempting to bring in a few extra tips. I'd taken the money Nikki had given me and bought some cute clothes for work.

I survey the area, looking for any sign of a home, aside from the place where I came from. Perhaps even a car, someone who can lend me their phone to call Luca for help.

The road is desolate down the mountainside.

The gravel is rough and worn as the switchbacks make it nearly impossible to see around the corner, not that I can see much. I keep to the edge of the road, the gravel under my shoes making it apparent that I'm following the road, as the grass is dried and dead under my feet.

If only it were summer, and at least then the sun might still be out.

I'm not overly tired, which either tells me it's not horribly late or the adrenaline surge is keeping me awake.

Luca must know by now that I'm missing, and I'm sure he's wracked with worry. Keeping to the edge of the road, I stumble through the dark. My arms are freezing, my fingers numb. As I finally reach the paved road at the bottom of the mountain, I'm shivering and clutching my arms to my chest to keep warm.

There's not a car in sight.

I walk.

The road is abandoned, and I'm not quite sure what road I'm on or where I am. The area unfamiliar in the dark, there are no landmarks, no signs, nothing recognizable yet.

Minutes feel like hours, and the headlights of a car in the distance gain on me. I keep to the edge of the road, not wanting to get hit. No one will stop if they can't see me. I wave my arms, hoping that the passerby will help.

They drive by at full speed before hitting their brakes and backing up, slowly approaching me.

The small sedan rolls down its window and I peek inside. "Harper, is that you?"

The young woman's voice, I barely recognize. But I've seen her before, I swear it.

"Do I know you?" I ask and shake away the cobwebs. "Can I get it a ride?"

"Of course." She unlocks the door, and I grab the handle, climbing into the front seat.

"Can I borrow your phone?" I ask, her face seemingly familiar as the interior lights flip on when I open the door.

But I'm not sure from where I recognize her.

She forces a smile as I buckle into the front seat, and she pulls onto the main road. "Where can I drop you off? You look lost. Did your car break down?"

She reaches into her purse and retrieves her cell phone, glancing at it briefly to unlock it before handing the device over to me.

"Thanks," I say and dial Luca. He picks up on the first ring.

"Hello?"

"Luca." My heart leaps wildly and my hands tremble. I'm unsure if it's the cold still raging through me or my anxiety rearing its ugly head.

"Harper! Where are you?"

My breath catches in my throat, and I hold back tears. Just hearing his voice offers me comfort. "I managed to escape. I'm in the car with—" I glance at the girl beside me. "What's your name again?"

"Izzie," she says, and her hands tighten on the steering wheel as she focuses on the road in front of her. "Where do you want me to drop you off?"

"She says her name is Izzie," I whisper and glance at her, realizing I recognize her and now remembering from where.

I'd met her once, briefly, outside of the police station. She'd handed me a business card with the name *Eagle Tactical*, had tried convincing me to talk to her dad who owned the company. I'd tossed the card and made sure Dante never knew about it.

"Where are you?" Luca asks.

"I'm not sure—I see the Blue Sky Resort. You can drop me off there," I say, glancing at Izzie, pointing at the bright lights and the resort in the distance on the mountain, wanting to be someplace public and safe.

Riding in the car with a stranger, after what just happened, I don't feel particularly safe.

She turns onto Great Mountain Road, which winds us up along the mountain. We're nowhere near the top, but it's a heavily traveled road, paved, unlike the one I'd been on when I'd escaped.

"Okay, Moreno and Nico aren't far. I'll have them pick you up. When you get there, go inside and stay in the lobby."

"I will. I love you, Luca."

"I love you too."

His words are like music to my ears, soothing

everything inside of me. But I know I'm not safe, not yet.

Jayden is still out there.

Izzie turns left onto the private road for the resort and she glances at me, her brow furrowed. I hand her back the phone. "Thanks."

"Listen, I didn't know—I'm sorry."

"You're sorry," I repeat slowly, wondering why she's apologizing. I shift uncomfortably in my seat as I glance her over.

Jayden had a partner.

There had been two people who'd grabbed me.

"You were there, with Jayden," I say and unbuckle my seatbelt.

"I didn't know—Jayden told me you were in on it. That you wanted to get away from the mafia. From Dante. When he mentioned your name, I believed him, because we'd met—outside the police station."

My breath catches in my throat and bile rises to my lips. I swallow the burning sensation down and gulp air with it. “You were the one who told him I’d gone to the cops.”

Izzie shakes her head, slowing down but approaching the resort. I reach for the door handle, yanking it open.

“I swear I only told my father. I had no idea Jayden was going to do that. I’m sorry, please, Harper, believe me.”

“He abducted me, and *you* helped him.”

Izzie’s eyes are wide, her bottom lip trembling. “I didn’t mean—I’m truly sorry.”

“If he ever comes near me again, I’ll see to it that you’re put behind bars along with him.”

She nods vigorously. “I swear on my life, I had no idea—he lied to me. Please, Harper, if you go to the police—”

She’s scared I’ll have her arrested for what she did, for her role in it, because Jayden couldn’t have done it on his own.

“Give me your phone,” I say, holding out my hand.

She nods, pushing it into my palm. “Whatever you want, it’s yours.”

“I’ll keep your little secret, on one condition.”

“Anything,” Izzie rasps.

“What’s your passcode?”

She relays it to me, and I unlock the phone, climbing out of the car.

“Is that it?” she asks, relief flooding her features.

Hardly.

“No.” I lean into the car, glaring at her. “One day, when I come looking for you, I’ll expect you to do as you’re told, no questions asked. You owe me.”

Izzie nods and tugs her bottom lip between her teeth.

“And you won’t breathe a word of your debt to anyone, including your father.”

“I swear it.”

I slam the car door and head inside the resort, finding the lobby. There are several patrons hanging around, and I grab a seat in an oversized chair near the fireplace.

A few sets of eyes glance at me, and I can't help but wonder how terrible I must look. I ignore all of them, sitting and dialing Luca.

"Harper?" his voice catches with worry.

"I kept Izzie's phone," I say matter of fact.

"Okay. Is she still there with you?" There's concern laced in his voice.

"No." I opt to keep her secret, even from Luca, for now. "Any idea how long until Moreno and Nico show up? The heat is on in this place, but I'm still chilly."

"They're twenty minutes out."

"How's Zeke?" I ask, glancing at the clock. I've been gone a couple of hours.

"He keeps asking for you. Nikki tucked him into bed already. I wanted to read him a story before bed, but I couldn't..."

I keep my voice down, not wanting anyone to

overhear my conversation with Luca. "It's okay. Give him an extra kiss from me, would you?"

"You can give him one yourself when you get home."

Exhaling a heavy sigh, I crack my neck. "Yeah. Listen, Jayden was completely foolish, snatching me from work, but his intentions weren't evil."

Luca scoffs. "Are you sure about that?" He doesn't sound convinced.

"Anyone who lays a finger on my wife—"

I cut him off. "Listen, I know you're mad. So am I, but this—it needs to end, now. Before someone gets hurt. You know your father will send men for retaliation. I don't want that."

"You're a better person than I am," Luca tells me. "But it's not up to you."

"Luca!"

I feel several sets of eyes on me, and I lower my voice again. "Please, talk to your father. Convince him that retribution isn't the only way."

I sense his frustration. "Do you honestly think he's going to listen to me?"

"He ought to if he wants you to run the organization one day." I glance toward the door and spot Moreno stalking inside, his overcoat on and black leather gloves. He looks warm.

He's also carrying my winter coat.

"Moreno's here," I say.

"Doesn't mean we have to hang up yet," Luca tells me cheekily. "Is it selfish that I don't want our call to end?"

"Not at all." I keep the phone to my ear as I stand and approach Moreno, taking the coat and sliding my arms one at a time through it. I button the jacket and he leads me back outside into the cold.

Moreno opens the door for me outside. The awaiting SUV is parked out front, the engine on, with Nico behind the wheel. Moreno opens the back door, and I climb inside.

"Where'd you get the phone?" Moreno asks, glancing at the device as he retrieves mine from his pocket.

"Just a girl who picked me up on the side of the road." I forgo giving her name to him.

He holds out his hand, wiggling his fingers, waiting for me to deposit it into his palm.

"Moreno wants the phone," I say, letting Luca know in case we get disconnected. "I'm talking to Luca."

"You can call him back on your phone." He ends the call for me, tossing the phone into the nearby garbage.

"Why did you do that?"

"I'm not about to let someone track you." He shoves my cell phone back into my hand. "Found this at the bar. Thought you might want it."

I climb into the backseat, and Moreno shuts the door for me. I dial Luca, not wanting to spend another minute apart.

"Everything okay?" he asks when he picks up the phone.

"Yeah, just Moreno being bossy and overbearing. He was worried Izzie might be tracking me."

"Izzie?" Moreno repeats, his curiosity piqued. "As in Isabel Monroe?" He glances at me from the front seat, turning around as much as possible to face me.

"She didn't give a last name," I say.

"Luca called and told us you got away. Did you see who the perpetrator was?" Moreno asks.

I'm quiet for a fraction of a second. "The two men wore masks," I say, opting not to start a war.

"Was the guy at the bar involved?" Moreno presses further. "Jayden Scott?"

"Moreno, I'm on the phone with Luca. Can we do this later?" I glare at him.

He clears his throat and shifts around to face forward. "Yeah, fine. We can do this with Dante when we get back to the compound."

Luca is quiet on the call for several seconds. "Are you okay?" he finally asks, breaking the silence when he realizes I'm no longer talking to Moreno.

"I'm..." I pause, trying to say exactly how I am, how I feel. I opt instead to answer with what we're doing. My emotions are a rollercoaster, and our conversation isn't the least bit private. "Just pulling away from the resort."

We head out of the resort, down the mountainous

winding road, and follow it south to Route 93, the main thoroughfare.

I hear Luca's sigh of relief. "I'm so glad you're okay. You are okay, right? Jayden didn't hurt you physically, touch you—"

"I'm okay," I say, reassuring him. "I was held in a basement, and I managed to sneak out through a window."

"Good. From now on, I want you to carry a gun with you, everywhere you go."

I laugh at his request. "Come on, Luca. That's not realistic. For starters, I'm not bringing a gun with me to school or when I'm carrying Zeke."

"We'll discuss it further when you get home."

I roll my eyes and tip my head back on the headrest. "You're so bossy tonight."

Luca fusses under his breath. "Am I?"

Like he can't tell? Maybe he's oblivious to it, but it's impossible for me to miss.

I glance out the window as we drive back onto the main road, and a shiver courses through me. It wasn't that long ago that I was walking on this road, alone, in the dark.

I pull my coat tighter.

"You're awfully quiet," Luca says.

"Just ... thinking," I confess.

He chuckles, sounding lighter, happier. "Don't do that too much, or you might give yourself a headache."

"Asshole," I joke with him, and then the air rushes out of my lungs in a scream.

A gunshot rings out through the vehicle out of nowhere.

The loud gunfire pierces my eardrums, making them ring as I grab the back door handle and yank at it.

It refuses to open.

Who the fuck child-locked the door?

I drop the phone. I can hear Luca's voice; he shouts out my name. It's distant and sounds far away in the chaos surrounding me.

"Moreno's been shot!" I scream, seeing him hunched forward, blood dripping from his head. "Nico shot him. I can't get out the back door."

"Shut up!" Nico shouts at me, and I lunge forward, wrapping my arms around his neck, choking him, trying to cut off his oxygen supply. He grabs at me with one arm, the SUV swerving on the road before he lifts the gun, shooting blindly at me.

Fuck.

The bullet misses, hitting the back window, shattering the glass in the trunk.

There's another way out.

I climb over the backseat and into the trunk, There's no interior handle, no release from the back that I can spot. I use my elbow, my coat protecting me as I break away the remaining of the shattered glass and pull the latch on the trunk from outside.

It doesn't budge with the doors locked.

Shit.

My only other option is to jump out the back window. We're moving at quite a fast clip, and I can't jump without risking severe injury.

Then again, getting shot is far worse.

There's a rough grumble.

"Moreno!" I shout, my eyes wide as I glance back at him. Is he still alive? I can't leave him with Nico.

"Who do you work for?" I shout at Nico and climb into the backseat, the best chance I have is if I can overtake Nico. Moreno needs medical attention.

"You'll find out soon enough." He chuckles, and my stomach plummets. "She'll be so excited that you're joining us."

She?

I can't even fathom who he's referring to, nor do I care.

"Now, sit in the back like a good little girl, Harper. I'd hate to have to bring you to her bruised and bloodied."

Glancing at the cell phone, it's still on, still counting the seconds that have passed by. Luca is on the line, probably listening to us. Good. Maybe he can figure out where Nico is taking us and have Dante intercept us before we get there.

"You're fucking insane if you think I'll do anything you tell me," I seethe at Nico. "Pull the fucking car over and get the hell out before I kill you."

He laughs, smirking as he glances back at me. "That's cute, buttercup. Thinking you have a chance. Moreno was your last chance, and he's dead."

I reach for his pulse, feeling it erratic, but he's still alive.

Blood seeps from the wound on his head, he seems to be unconscious, bent forward, the seatbelt restraining him.

Moreno has to have a gun on him. I climb over the console, making my way into the front passenger seat.

"What the hell—Harper?" Nico snarls at me and lifts his gun. "Get in the back!"

My fingers graze over Moreno's holster and I grab the gun, cocking off the trigger and shooting round after round into Nico.

Except there's no bullets.

Nico laughs darkly and smiles wickedly as he

glances at me. "Did you really think I'd let Moreno carry a loaded gun?"

"What? How?" I climb over Moreno's body, and Nico is grabbing my hair, yanking me out of the seat.

My fingers itch on the doorhandle, so close, I can almost yank it open.

If I can get out, then Nico will be forced to stop. Forced to abandon the car and chase me. He'll leave Moreno alone, and maybe Dante and Luca can find me.

It's my best hope. The darkness of night is the only chance I have at getting away.

I pull the latch, the front door swinging open, and I jump haphazardly onto the ground.

It fucking burns.

Every inch of my body is like fire licking my skin. My black pants are torn, shredded from the jump, and my coat took the brunt over my arms and chest, tearing but not destroying it.

I stumble into the forest, hearing the screech of tires and the engine alive and idling as Nico jumps out and chases after me.

Can I outsmart him? If I run through the forest, I can lose him, and then get back to the vehicle, and I can leave his ass behind.

I run through the woods, hearing him give chase to me, his feet not far behind as he catches up to me with long strides.

Nico is taller, giving himself an advantage, and I do my best not to run in a straight line, trying to avoid him catching me. But it does little use.

He's gaining on me, and fast.

His footfalls aren't the least bit silent, and neither are mine. I'm gasping for breath, making my location far too obvious.

I need to try something else, something different, because I can't outrun him and he's gaining on me, fast.

I skirt around a larger tree, climbing it, holding my breath so he can't find me, spot me.

I get halfway up to the nearest branch, sling my leg up and over when it snaps, landing me flat on my back.

Nico chuckles, staring right down at me. “Welcome back.” He lifts me with ease, tossing me over his shoulder, carrying me back to the vehicle. He grabs a set of zip ties from the glovebox and yanks them on my arms, shoving me into the backseat.

This feels all too familiar.

FIVE

LUCA

From silence to the sweet symphony of her voice.

She's alive.

"Where are you taking me?"

The voice through the phone is slightly muffled, and there's a strange sound before it becomes a bit clearer.

"Where are you taking me?" Harper asks again, this time with more grit.

"Shut up!" Nico shouts.

I'm careful not to say a word until I put my phone on mute, listening as I allow her conversation to be on speakerphone for Ashton and Dante to hear.

I grabbed Dante the moment chaos ensued with Nico.

"Take a car out toward Blue Sky Resort, see if you can intercept them," Dante orders. "Call me the minute you find out anything."

Ashton and I head out together. There are other men of Dante's, but learning of Nico's betrayal, it's clear as day he's unsure who he can trust.

I don't know what he intends to do with his men.

Interrogate them.

I'd punish each of them until they come clean with the truth.

I don't wait around to find out. Ashton and I are in the vehicle, already on our way, the phone on speaker and mute, so that we can hear every word, every gasp and plea through the phone.

It's agonizing to listen and not be able to do anything.

But our silence is the only way to save her.

Nico can't know that we're listening in and Harper is doing her damndest to relay as much information as she can, without making it obvious.

"At least drop off Moreno at the hospital," Harper pleads. "You can take me, do whatever you want, but don't let Moreno die."

I glance at Ashton, relieved that he's still alive.

"That would waste valuable time," Nico says.

"Then leave him on the side of the road," Harper says. "Let someone else deal with him. Isn't that better for you—not to have to clean up his dead body?"

I grimace, praying that she'll give me more information. My foot is like lead on the gas, and while I drive, Ashton texts Dante with any new pertinent information.

Right now, there isn't much. But if Moreno gets dumped on the side of the road, we're not going to have time to take him to the hospital and chase after Nico to rescue Harper.

I'll always choose Harper first.

"His dead body makes little difference to me. You, on the other hand, bringing you in alive brings me a sweet deal."

I glance at Ashton, unpleased with this little bit of information from Nico.

"What kind of deal?" Harper asks the question I want to know as well.

"You'll just have to wait and see." Nico laughs a dark and sinister snigger that sends my stomach plummeting.

Silence ensues between Nico and Harper.

"Please," Harper begs, "drop Moreno off at the hospital."

"I have a better idea," Nico says, and silence follows.

There's the slamming of a car door.

"Luca, if you can hear me, we just pulled over. Nico got out of the car. We're still on Route 93 heading south."

For an instant, I unmute my device. "I can hear you," I say, but I'm unsure if she can hear me. She doesn't respond, indicating she can.

"Luca? Is that you? I can barely hear you. Shit, he's —" she grows quiet. "What are you doing with Moreno?" Harper asks.

Ashton mutes our end of the call.

There's the obvious slam of a car door. "Let me go!"

It sounds like she's fighting him off. We're half an hour out at best.

"Get off me!"

The door slams shut and then it does so again.

"Luca, he just dumped Moreno on the side of the road!"

Ashton retrieves his phone, smirking when he pulls up Harper's location, showing it to me.

"How long have you been tracking *my wife*?" I sneer in disgust.

"Since Dante put a tracker on her phone. The first night they met."

Shaking my head, I should be angry about the betrayal, but I'm grateful knowing that so long as they have battery power and cell service, we'll know where they are.

"Text Dante, let him know where they stopped and dropped Moreno off."

He taps at his phone, silent, and sighs.

"What?" I glance at him. Clearly, Dante sent him a text in response.

"You're not going to like this," Ashton says, his expression grim. "He wants us to pick up Moreno and drop him off at the hospital. Since we have a location on Harper, she's secondary priority."

"Secondary priority, my ass. I'm not—"

Ashton types something quickly into his phone, and then it rings. He puts it on speaker for me to hear.

"Luca, you're picking up Moreno. This isn't up for discussion." Dante is curt in his demand, to the point. "You're the nearest and you have the exact location."

"Ashton can drop you a pin and someone else can grab Moreno."

"I don't trust anyone else right now, Luca."

"Fuck!" I slam my fist against the steering wheel. "Nico has Harper, I can't let them get away."

"We won't. I've got Liam and Sophia en route to the compound to assist."

I glance at Ashton. "That's not good enough. You're bringing in the two newest recruits to what—exactly?"

"Luca, understand that I'm as troubled by her abduction and betrayal as you are."

"You never even liked Harper!" I shout through the phone. "You're probably relieved your little problem has been taken care of."

I hit the gas pedal harder, wanting to get to Moreno quickly so that we can continue to go find Harper.

"On the contrary, I find her quite ... admirable. She's certainly kept up her end of the bargain. Keeping our secret, which reminds me, we have a location on Harper."

I huff under my breath. "I'm aware, Ashton told me a few minutes ago about the tracker you installed on her phone."

"Yes, but we also know where Nico is taking her. Pick up Moreno, head to the hospital, and I'll meet you there."

"No. I can't risk Nico getting too far ahead. I'll drop off Moreno, but I can't stop for a chitchat." I grind and hit the gas harder.

"Up here!" Ashton tells me when he tracks the location on the phone. "He should be somewhere nearby."

I slow the vehicle, keeping an eye on both the road and the grass nearby.

Ashton points several yards up ahead. "Over there!"

I flip the hazard lights on. They flash as I put the vehicle in park, and we hurry to get Moreno off the side of the road and into the backseat. We lay him down, his body motionless, but he's still got a pulse.

I'm not sure whether he can hear us or not. He appears to be unconscious. His eyes are closed, he doesn't so much as make a sound, but he's alive, for now.

"Hang in there," Ashton says to Moreno. "Nova will kill me if anything happens to you."

SIX

NOVA

"Where is he?" I rush through the double doors, demanding to see my father. My mother is just a few short steps behind me, trying to keep pace, but I'm practically running to the front desk, demanding to know where they've taken my father.

The woman at the front desk is absolutely no help.

I want to lunge across the desk and strangle her. I swear she's got her finger ready on the panic button, and I spin around when I hear my name.

"Nova!" Ashton's voice is music to my ears. "We need a gurney!" He grunts as his arms are beneath my father's and Luca has my dad's legs, carrying him inside.

Luca is double parked outside the ambulance bay. There are nearby wheelchairs accessible, but I have a feeling Dad will fall right out of one in his unconscious state.

"Moreno!" Mom rushes to Dad's aid, but there isn't much she can do.

Hospital staff see the injury, the way Luca and Ashton are carrying my father inside, and they immediately grab a gurney, helping put him onto it before ushering him back behind the double doors, leaving us in the waiting room.

"We need one of you to give us his name and medical information," a gentleman says, and Mom nods, following him.

Ashton glances from the double doors to me. For a moment, I think he might step forward, embrace me, tell me everything will be okay, and I'll take comfort in those words.

But then I remember we're not anything.

He's not mine.

We're broken up.

It's like a knife to my gut when I've already been poisoned and gasping for my last breath.

"Ashton, we have to go," Luca's voice pulls me from my reverie.

"Go?" I shake my head at Luca. "You're just dropping him off and leaving?"

Hearing that hurts worse than the phantom knife.

If Ashton leaves with Luca, I'll never forgive him.

"I have to go get Harper." Luca stares at me for a fraction of a second. "Are you coming?" He glances back at Ashton as he walks backward toward the exit of the hospital and toward his awaiting vehicle.

"I have orders," Ashton says, grabbing his phone from his pocket. "As do you." He walks outside and I can't help but wonder if I'll never see him again.

Standing outside the car, it looks like Luca and Ashton are arguing.

I can't make out the words being exchanged, and I walk away; it doesn't matter.

I can't do a damned thing to help Harper.

I hate waiting. Standing on my feet, pacing back and forth while my father is in the emergency room getting tended to by physicians, and I'm not allowed past the double doors while they take care of him.

Rolling my lips together, I stifle the tears, keeping them at bay.

"Nova, sweetie, why don't you take a seat?" Mom's voice is soft. She glances up at me, the pain obvious on her face.

Looking at her makes me want to bawl.

I glance away, glaring at Ashton who is covered in blood, his shirt stained crimson from carrying my father's lifeless body inside the hospital.

It's an image I don't think I can ever unsee. He glances at his phone, wanders outside to take the call. He doesn't so much as look at me, touch me.

He barely even acknowledges my existence.

Halsey storms into the building like he owns the place. Not only is he capo, but he's Moreno's cousin. There's pain written all over his face, even though I see he tries to hide it behind his tough exterior.

I half expect him to storm up to the desk and demand an update.

No.

He approaches my mother and takes a seat beside her.

I can't help but overhear their conversation.

"Any word yet?" Halsey asks, his expression grim.

Mom shakes her head and sniffles. Her hands are trembling as she grips a wrinkled tissue in her hand.

Halsey glances around, taking everything in. Surveying the exits, the staff, every person who enters and leaves the emergency room waiting area. His glances are calculated, the timing impeccable, like he's constantly on high alert.

A guard dog.

Does he think that Nico will be back to finish the job and take out my father? Halsey can't protect my dad from out here.

But he doesn't seem to be barging in past the double doors.

"Have a seat," Halsey says to me, gesturing to a chair.

"No, thanks." I can't sit still. I feel like if I do, I might actually break.

"That wasn't a question." Halsey glares at me, and I glance toward the ambulance bay and ignore Halsey, stalking outside into the cold autumn air to find Ashton.

He's been gone a few minutes, and I'm done dealing with Halsey.

I'm not mafia. I don't have to take orders from them.

Halsey grumbles and follows me toward the exit, but he doesn't leave the building. I turn around, raising an eyebrow when I catch him glancing at my mother and then back at me.

Strange.

My stomach somersaults, and the anxiety I've been feeling since the moment I learned of Harper's disappearance has been gnawing at me.

"Shouldn't you be helping look for Harper?" I glare at him.

Halsey sighs and folds his arms across his chest. "Not my job." He doesn't move from his position, keeping a watchful eye on the two of us.

Well, fuck him.

I saunter around the corner outside, barreling into Ashton. "She's not going to like that, sir."

Not going to like what?

Who is he talking to?

Dante?

Another minute, and he ends the call, Ashton shoving the phone into his pocket. He grabs my wrist and drags me back into the hospital.

"Oww, what are you doing?" I yank my arm free. It isn't like he hurt me, not physically, but his touch right now, it's giving me mixed signals, as is that intense, heated gaze behind those dark eyes.

"Protecting you," Ashton says.

"I don't need your protection," I sneer and head past him, back out the doors and into the cold.

My jacket is beside Mom's seat, and I don't dare admit I'm freezing. At least I'm wearing a long, dusty-rose cardigan, but it's not warm enough for today's chill.

Ashton groans at me, removes his leather coat and slings it over my shoulders. "Dante wants you to have a bodyguard until this thing with Harper is resolved."

"This thing—you mean her kidnapping?" I shoot him a nasty look. "I'm honestly shocked you didn't go with Luca and decided to stay here."

"Luca is back at the compound, with Dante."

I stare at him like he's sporting a halo, my mafia devil. "Why would he be there? Harper is missing."

"We have her location, and I hung up the call with her to conserve battery power on her phone. Dante thinks he's taking her all the way to Las Vegas."

"You're just going to let Nico take her there?" I keep walking, my legs growing cold, filled with a dull ache, but I slide my arms into Ashton's coat that he lent me.

If he's cold, he gives no indication of his discomfort.

"He's getting a plane ready to get a team there upon her arrival."

"A team? Dante doesn't know who he can trust." I stop walking and shiver.

Ashton pulls me closer. Grabbing the lapels of his jacket, he zips the leather up for me to keep warm. "He knows he can trust Luca, Liam, and me. The others—he's interrogating himself."

I expel a heavy breath, glad I'm not in the house right now.

"Is Luca helping with the interrogation?" If he went home at Dante's insistence, then is he part of the brutal methods that Dante will employ?

"Probably," Ashton whispers. "Does it matter? His methods are tough, but they work."

I laugh darkly under my breath. "They work so well that there was a traitor right under Dante's nose and he never even knew."

Ashton ignores my remark. "I got word from Dante that Rhys is set to return tomorrow. Flying him in first thing tomorrow morning."

"He is?" A tiny smile forms at the corners of my lips. I've always felt a connection with Rhys. He'd been my bodyguard all those years growing up, protecting me. We'd practically become friends.

"Don't look so happy."

Is that jealousy I see? I tilt my head, staring up, wishing I could read his thoughts. I lift my arm to run my fingers through his hair, and he grabs my wrist.

"What are you doing, Nova?"

"Touching you," I whisper, which is apparently not the right response.

He shakes his head. "You don't get to do that, not after breaking up with me."

I inhale sharply. "Fine." I take a step back and cross the street, farther from the hospital. I quicken my pace to get away from him. The cold stings my cheeks, my eyes burn with tears, and I worry they might actually freeze to my eyelashes as they water.

"Nova!" he calls, hurrying to catch up with me after traffic passes, and he's jogging until he finally reaches my strides, walking in pace with me.

"What? Just go back to the hospital or go back to Dante." I shrug away from him as he grabs my arm, and I refuse to meet his stare as I wipe a stray tear, praying he doesn't notice.

If he does, I'll blame it on the frigid temperatures.

I'm not crying.

"I have orders."

That stops me dead in my tracks. "What?"

"I have orders."

"I heard what you said." I turn around to face him.

"Are you—crying?" he asks and there's concern laced in his tone. His bottom lip is pouty and I try not to meet his intense dark gaze that is unwavering.

I glance away, staring at another couple who are walking together, bundled for this weather, unlike the two of us. They're wearing winter beanies, scarves, gloves, and heavy down jackets. I force a smile as they nod.

After they pass, I snarl up at Ashton. "Quit changing the subject. What are your orders?"

Ashton glances me over from head to toe. "You."

I shake my head, taken aback by his answer. "What does that mean?" Is he giving me some stupid riddle or being serious?

"Dante wants me to be your bodyguard until Rhys returns tomorrow. It's just for a day," he says, like that will make it okay. "And besides, it's already late. Not even a full twenty-four hours we have to do this."

"I don't have to do anything," I scoff at him and hurry away.

SEVEN

ASHTON

Chasing after Nova in the dark is like chasing a firefly that keeps escaping your grasp. Tenacious.

I'm on her heels, following her every step as she briskly keeps pace ahead of me. I could easily catch up, but I'm tasked with being her bodyguard, so staying behind her and watching our surroundings is preferred.

"I don't have to do anything," she shouts at me, not liking that I've told her the truth, that I'm her new bodyguard until Rhys returns.

Rhys, who was supposed to be retired, with a permanent job watching Rylan, who is now entrusted with another family on the island. Dante informed me that he and Rhys worked quickly to have Rylan rehomed and given a new guardian, a teacher at his school.

It leaves a sour taste, the idea of rehoming a child. Rylan is not a pet, and yet, we need the extra manpower and support. Dante trusts Rhys, which means I do as well.

"Except, you do," I say, and I know she'll hate me for it, but I still remind her of the truth. "You don't get a choice." She's the daughter of a second in command. She's as much mafia whether she wants to be or not.

She can't walk away from that life, no matter how hard she tries.

And boy, does she try.

Nova stops walking and turns around to face me. "No, you don't get a choice!" she shouts, and then spins on her heel and continues walking, taking the loop that inevitably leads us back to the hospital.

I let her scream, because if that's what makes her feel better right now, she can shout at me all she wants.

Her father is dying.

I'm surprised the man is still breathing and his heart is still beating after the bullet to the head.

I see where Nova gets her fighting spirit from.

She doesn't say another word to me, and I can't quite read if it's out of anger, annoyance, or hatred as she storms back into the hospital.

Halsey looks relieved to see us. I'm sure he's aware of my new bodyguard position with Nova. It's temporary, at least, and while I'd love for it to help rekindle what we had between us, the girl looks at me like I'm a dagger intent on being plunged into her heart.

I never want to hurt Nova.

I didn't when I told her the truth, that I fully intend on working for my father after graduation. I can't help that she didn't like the truth. I would have thought she'd have realized as much, seeing as who her father is, but that was my mistake.

And now, the truth has cost me *her*.

She slumps down into the chair beside Paige, her mother, and I'm grateful to just be inside, out of the cold. My long-sleeved shirt did little to keep me warm, and only now do I feel the shiver crawl down my spine from the cold.

I stalk to the vending machine and grab myself a coffee. It's bitter and strong, but the heat from the cup helps warm my hands.

My heart, on the other hand, I'm not sure anything will ever warm that up again.

There's little good news.

Moreno is in a coma. Paige and Nova are at his bedside, Halsey stands outside the door, making sure only those who are hospital staff or family come into his room.

I keep watch outside the hall, nearby if Nova needs me but far enough to give her space. She finally saunters out into the hallway, her eyelids heavy.

"I'm ready to go home."

"Of course, I'll drive you."

Halsey tosses me his car keys, letting me drive the vehicle back to the compound with my charge.

She's my responsibility, getting her home safely.

And I don't take that job lightly.

I wrap an arm around her waist, holding her to me, and she lolls her head onto my shoulder for a fraction of a second while we walk to the elevator. The warmth floods through me like fire; she pulls away, perhaps feeling it too.

Yawning, she straightens her shoulders, acting like she's awake.

It's nearly four in the morning.

I'm exhausted.

I can only imagine how she must be feeling.

There's been no word on Harper. I've checked the location on the tracker, and her phone is still heading south on Route 93. Dante seems to be right, she's heading toward Las Vegas, assuming she's still in the vehicle and hasn't fled on foot.

But she's made no attempt to contact any of us; if she had, Luca would have told me by now.

With the headstart, we can't catch up to Harper by car.

Dante is working to get us access to a private plane to Vegas in the morning. It's at least a fifteen-hour drive plus stops for gas.

Fighting sleep, I drive us back to the compound. It doesn't take long for me to hear Nova softly snoring in the front seat. When I get back to the house, I carefully unbuckle her and carry her inside.

She stirs slightly. "Ashton?" The way she whispers my name sends my heart pounding.

Not now.

Inwardly, I grumble at myself for feeling anything at a time like this.

"I've got you," I whisper and carry her inside and up the flight of stairs to her bedroom.

I'm surprised that she doesn't fight me. Her arms are warm around my neck and she curls into me, as though we fit perfectly together.

Laying her down on her bed, I remove her shoes and she fumbles out of her coat, tossing it to the floor. Nova climbs under the covers. "Stay with me, please."

Against better judgment, I oblige, removing my shoes and jacket.

Nova makes room, scooting farther back on the bed, shuffling toward the wall while I climb under the covers with her.

It takes no time at all for me to fall asleep. I'm exhausted and knowing that I'm in Nova's bed, no one will get to her because they'd have to get through me first.

EIGHT

LUCA

I barge into Ashton's room. His bed is untouched, but I haven't seen him at all this morning. Weird.

I grab my phone and text Halsey.

Me: Is Ashton with you?

It only takes a few seconds for him to respond to my text message.

Halsey: No, I gave him the car around 4am. Did he not make it home?

Me: I'm checking.

I move from one room to the next and then open Nova's door without so much as a knock. If she came in after four with Ashton, I don't necessarily need to wake her up. I do, however, need to find Ashton.

Ashton's arms are curled around Nova, her back to him, eyes closed. Both are sound asleep. Too bad I'm the one who has to wake his ass up after a couple of measly hours of sleep. He got more than I did.

I'm running on fumes.

And lots of coffee.

"Wake up, asshole. We've got a flight to catch."

Ashton groans and rubs the sleep from his eyes. "What about the bodyguard detail?" he grumbles and rolls onto his back.

Nova pulls the covers up over her head, clearly not ready to wake up yet.

"Rhys got in twenty minutes ago. He's taking over your duties." Ashton should be relieved, given their recent breakup.

Although I know he's still pining over Nova.

And after catching them in bed together this morning, I don't know what's going on, and I don't need to know.

"Fuck," he mumbles and pushes himself out of bed. "I'm awake."

He looks more like a dead man walking, or maybe a zombie, but I leave the bedroom door open and walk away.

Ashton clears his throat and heads out of Nova's bedroom, heading for his room to get dressed.

I make my way down the stairs, hurrying to the kitchen. My phone buzzes and I glance at the text from Halsey.

Halsey: Did you find them? Or do we have two more missing persons?

Me: They were in bed ... together.

Halsey: Knew he couldn't last ten minutes without her.

I roll my eyes and shove my phone back into my pocket. Ashton and Nova's love life isn't my concern. I rub the back of my neck. Funny, considering last year I nearly killed him for hooking up with her.

"Morning." Rhys nods at me as he pours himself a cup of coffee.

"Surprised to see you back here." I never thought I'd see him again, especially from what I'd heard about him looking after the boy Dante had abducted.

"Yeah, me too." Rhys laughs nervously. "I was really enjoying those margaritas on the beach."

"Retirement too boring?" I joke, and Dante breezes around the corner.

"On the contrary, I know without a doubt Rhys is loyal. I can't say that about all of my men."

Exhaling a heavy breath, I nod. "Did any of them crack?" I ask, needing to know if Nico was the only leak inside Dante's organization.

Dante shakes his head, his brow pinching with frustration. "None of them so much as knew Nico was a traitor to the family or where they were taking Harper."

"Are you sure she's en route to Vegas?" I ask, still uncertain about the location on her phone. It could have been intentionally misleading us.

"Livia DeLuca has a residence in Las Vegas; she's the current head of the DeLuca operations, from what intel I've gathered. And this morning, I discovered my mole was found dead. Bullet wound to the head. I shouldn't be surprised that they're coming after my family."

"You think that's what this is, retribution for having someone on the inside?" I'm not entirely convinced; it could just as easily be revenge. Harper shot and killed Livia's husband, Santino. "Livia and Santino were married."

"I'm not denying that, but it's why I put a bodyguard detail on Nova. I wouldn't put it past Livia to come after my girls."

"Your girls?" I repeat, surprised by his remark. Harper is mafia, but Nova, she's never wanted anything to do with her father, same as me. She shouldn't be tied up in this mess.

"My family," Dante says, and waves a hand dismissively. "If Livia wants to get to me, she'll go after Harper, Nova, Paige, and Nikki." He stares at me. "I know you can handle your own and you'll have Ashton and Liam accompanying you to Vegas."

"Liam is coming with us?" I rub my eyes, exhausted, and know that I'll need to focus. I can't let Harper down. "Are you sure he's ready for that?"

"I need a full team I can count on, and Liam, as well as Sophia, aren't familiar faces to the DeLucas."

"Liam's been living with us the entire time," I remind Dante. "It's possible they already have a dossier on him and would know he has a twin."

"Well the fuck aware," Dante growls. "But our options are limited, and I need you to infiltrate their organization, not just waltz in and shoot up the place to get Harper back."

I huff under my breath. "We're not going undercover."

We don't have time to fuck around and find Harper.

"You'll do exactly as I say, because I've been in this situation before, with your mother."

Has he lost his mind? "When?"

"Before you were born. It's not something your mother or I ever discuss, but I know how the DeLucas operate. I'm sure some things have changed, but the fact they've taken Harper all the way to Vegas tells me that some things are exactly the same."

Rhys finishes his coffee. "Are you sure I can't be of help?" he asks Dante. "If Nova remains inside the compound, she'll be safe."

"You don't know Moreno's daughter as well as I thought if you believe she'll listen to a word of my demands."

I force the smile away.

Rhys nods and laughs. "Yeah, she's got the willpower of Moreno all right. Speaking of Moreno—how is he doing?"

Ashton hurries down the stairs, and I hear his footsteps approaching the kitchen.

"Still no word yet," Dante says. "But I'll keep everyone updated as soon as we have news."

"Do I have time to grab coffee before we head out?" Ashton fights back a yawn, failing miserably.

"There will be coffee on the plane," Dante says. "Get to the car. We're only a few minutes from the airfield."

Dread weighs heavily on me. It only gets worse when my phone rings and it's Harper's parents calling. I'm slipping on my shoes, and I really want to chuck my phone across the room.

But I try to maintain some semblance of sanity, or I worry that I'll be forced to stay behind with Nova.

"Are you going to answer that?" Ashton asks, glancing at my phone in my hand.

"It would be best if you don't," Dante grumbles at me.

"Right." I send the call to voicemail and grab my coat.

They call again.

Apparently, me not answering doesn't mean anything to them.

By the third time, I grumpily answer the call. "What?" I bite out, unable to stop myself. Blame it on my lack of sleep, but talking to her parents who despise me, isn't at the top of my agenda this morning. Rescuing Harper, however, is.

"That's no way to greet your mother-in-law," Catrina says.

I would apologize if I cared about her feelings, but my thoughts are entirely on Harper. “I’m busy.”

“Clearly,” Catrina says, miffed. “Some strange man answered Harper’s phone.”

“What man?” I pause and feel the breath stolen right out of me.

“I don’t know. I was assuming it was one of your friends.” She huffs. “He sounded angry and hung up on me. Harper now won’t answer her phone, and I wanted to find out about holiday plans.”

Ashton takes the keys from me and gestures for me to get into the vehicle while he drives us to the airfield. “Now isn’t a good time, Catrina.”

My stomach sinks. If Catrina called and Nico answered the phone, then he must have found her phone. Her location is as good as useless now.

Even if they don’t know without a doubt that there’s a tracker in her phone, they’ll suspect it. Nico may be a traitor, but he isn’t an idiot.

I climb into the backseat, letting Liam ride shotgun with Ashton.

Sophia sits in the backseat with me, and I glance at the door as Nova comes barreling outside, pulling her coat on and carrying her shoes. “Wait for me!”

Rhys is cursing under his breath. “I swear she never listens.”

“I’m not staying behind. If they’re going to rescue Harper, I’m coming with them.”

“What was that about rescuing my daughter?” Catrina balks, overhearing some part of Nova’s outburst. I’m really hoping it was the last bit about coming with and nothing else.

“I have to go.” I abruptly end the call, hanging up on Catrina.

I can’t tell her the truth, and I hope she doesn’t keep calling and pestering me for answers.

Rhys grabs a set of keys from the house. “Nova, you’re riding with me.”

“I swear if you take me someplace else—”

“Relax. Anyone else want to ride with us?” Rhys offers and Sophia climbs out of the backseat. “I’ll join you.”

While they're playing games picking who rides in what vehicle, I'm grumbling and growing more irritated with every passing second. "Can we go already?"

Ashton waits until Rhys is out of the way and then hits the gas, using GPS to take us to the small airstrip nearby.

I've never had the luxury of riding on a private plane, and to be honest, I really hope I don't have to do this ever again. One abduction is far too many.

I board the airplane, and as if on cue, Jack, Harper's father, calls me. I send the call straight to voicemail and shut off my phone. It's not like I can do much with it on during the flight. Dante has assured me that he'll let me know if Harper reaches out during the short flight —he has my phone being transferred directly to him.

That will be boatloads of fun if Jack and Catrina keep pestering Dante.

Let him deal with Harper's parents. I don't have it in me to pretend that everything is all right.

I can barely sit still, my knee bouncing with anxiety as the plane takes off. I'm not a nervous flyer.

It has nothing to do with the plane and everything to do with my concern for *my wife*. Dante has given us weapons, ammunition, and we have Rhys accompanying us. Of the entire group, he's the one with the most experience, but his expertise has been playing bodyguard to Nova for all those years growing up.

It doesn't exactly scream confidence when we're running into a gunfight.

Ashton is seated across from me, glaring at Rhys across the aisle. "What's your problem?" Rhys asks.

Ashton's eyes flicker and he doesn't say a word.

His hands grip the armrests and his nostrils flare.

Is he—jealous?

Ashton doesn't have to worry; nothing is going to happen between Rhys and Nova.

Once we've reached cruising altitude, Ashton stands and stalks across the aisle, hovering over Rhys, who is seated next to Nova. "You're in my seat."

Rhys straightens his shoulders and takes a long, slow look at Ashton. "And. Your point?"

Nova unclasps her seatbelt and pushes past both of them. “Take my seat.”

Ashton reaches for Nova’s arm, but she pulls away before he can touch her, stalking toward the back of the plane. The private jet isn’t that large, and she sits next to Sophia in the aisle seat.

Ashton follows Nova, not taking a hint, and I glance over my shoulder as he sits behind me, directly across from her.

Ashton keeps his voice low, and I lean back, trying not to overhear their conversation. “Can we talk?”

So much for any ounce of privacy.

“No!” she shouts at him.

NINE

NOVA

Why won't Ashton leave me the hell alone? It's not bad enough Dante forced him yesterday to be my damn bodyguard, but I just can't deal with him today.

My mind is on my father, but sitting around a hospital room all day, what good would that do?

Harper is still in trouble, and I can't believe Dante didn't send an actual team to help bring her back. He sent the fucking recruits instead of the cavalry.

Does he want Harper to stay missing?

Maybe he wants her dead.

Wouldn't surprise me. The bastard never liked her anyhow.

Ashton reaches across the aisle, our seats facing each other, and while I do my best to look anywhere but at him, his eyes are locked on me.

"Are you going to ignore me forever?" Ashton asks, his hands folded together in his lap.

Sophia unbuckles her seatbelt.

"Where are you going?" My voice raises an octave when I see her stand.

Liam's sister gives me an apologetic look before taking my seat next to Rhys.

"Wow," I mutter, shocked that she's siding with Ashton.

He doesn't even miss a beat, switching seats from across from me, moving right into Sophia's seat, sitting next to me.

"Happy?" I retort, seeing that he got exactly what he wanted.

"Am I happy that we're broken up and you can barely look at me, let alone talk to me? No." He doesn't reach for me, doesn't so much as touch me, but he does sit close enough that I can feel his presence like a raging heat that makes me sweat.

"What do you want?" I finally shift my body to face him. "We're not getting back together."

"Wasn't asking, sweetheart."

I snarl at his nickname. "Don't sweetheart me. I'm not your anything." My words are intended to cut him, but he doesn't so much as flinch.

"Well, not yet," he says and smiles with that boyish grin that used to make me weak at the knees. It probably landed all those other girls in his bed, too.

I force away all feelings and fold my arms across my chest. "What do you want to talk about? Other than us."

He raises an eyebrow. "Us?"

"I'm not talking about us," I reiterate.

"You're the one who brought it up." Ashton is all smiles, that dimple making its world-class debut, and I want to wipe it right off his face. He's fucking playing with me and enjoying every second.

My eyes tighten and I inhale sharply. "Well, fuck. Why don't we talk about you? If you want to talk, that is." I can't help the anger in my voice or the annoyance that he's paying attention to me when he should be worried about Harper or even my father, Moreno.

Ashton seems to relax with that topic in mind. "I'm an open book." He stretches his arms, casually putting one behind my headrest, and I pry his arm away and back to his side.

"You're an ass."

He doesn't appear to be bothered by my insult. "Yell at me all you want, Nova. I know you're hurting."

"You hurt me!" How does he not see that he's the reason I'm angry with him? Does he think it's because my best friend was kidnapped and my father was shot and is in a coma? Ashton and I were fighting long before Harper was taken.

He's quiet, and for once, I don't have any idea what he's thinking.

I glance away, staring out the window, my eyes burning, threatening me with tears that I refuse to shed in front of him. The last thing I want is for

Ashton to see me cry. I bite down on my bottom lip, hoping the pain will stop the emotional torture.

His hand is warm, gentle, soft as he grazes my arm to get my attention.

I should shuck him off me, but I don't. Just like last night, having him in my bed was comforting. My eyes shut, avoiding so much as looking at him as I face the open window shade of the jet, and I know if we were seated anywhere else, he'd be pulling me onto his lap, cradling me.

I'm grateful for the individual leather seat, keeping him from scooting over next to me, forcing our bodies to touch.

I keep my back to him. One hand is on my arm, the other tangles in the nape of my neck, massaging my scalp, tugging my hair slightly, and fuck, his touch is a turn-on. The way his hands command my body, making my insides warm and tingly.

I hate him for it.

I want to scream at him to get off of me, but the words don't come.

Anger sizzles in silence to nothingness.

His hand keeps kneading my neck, fisting my hair, tugging in a sensual maneuver that sends my pussy pulsating.

My breathing deepens and grows raspier. I pray he doesn't notice the change, the intensity from anger to arousal.

I feel his presence, the heat of his body as he leans forward, his breath against my ear. "Want to join the mile-high club?"

For a fraction of a second, a tiny smile reaches my lips because, yes, I really do. But I shove it down and spin around, pushing him backward out of my personal space, including my seat. "In your dreams."

Ashton smirks, and I want so desperately to reach across and wipe that smug grin off his face. "You're always in my dreams, babe."

I pull back my fist to land a blow for calling me *babe* when we're broken up, and he grabs my wrist, stopping me. "When did you become so violent?" He's taunting me. "For someone who wants nothing to do with the mafia, you seem quite—invested."

"Because my father is dying and my best friend is missing!"

I wince when I feel multiple sets of eyes on me. Those who aren't glancing back at me are definitely listening. It's not like I've been quiet this flight.

I grumble under my breath, unbuckle my seatbelt and stalk to the restroom at the back of the airplane.

It's the only place I can get a little peace and quiet without Ashton interfering.

Correction.

Someone is knocking on the door to the bathroom.

"Seriously?" Can't he take a hint and leave me the hell alone?

"It's Rhys." There's another knock. "You okay, or do you want me to knock some sense into him?"

I slowly open the bathroom door, offering a weak smile. "I'm okay." I'm not sure I'm convincing him, and I definitely am not convincing myself I'm fine. I'm a mess! I meet his gaze for a fraction of a second before I gesture for him to step aside because he's blocking the aisle.

"You know, Dante hired me to protect you. That includes from college-aged boys and ex-boyfriends."

I chuckle under my breath. "I really doubt that's why Dante brought you back."

"He wants me as your full-time bodyguard," Rhys says, and I nod slowly. I always liked Rhys. Not in a romantic, love interest type of way, more like he let me sneak off and get away with practically anything. And as far as I know, he never told Dad the shit I got into.

"Yeah, full-time until Harper is home." I'm not entirely surprised, a little that Rhys is back, but Dante and Dad have always trusted him with their lives and with mine.

Rhys gives me that *if you say so* stare, and I can't help but cock my head. "Do you know something you're not telling me?"

He laughs under his breath. "I know a lot of things, none of which are leaving this mouth." He points at his lips. "Besides, I heard you have no interest in joining the family business. Surprised Dante even let you on this flight."

"Do you think I gave him a choice?" I don't remember getting an invite. I heard Luca and Ashton were jetting to Vegas, and I joined them.

Rhys chuckles and steps aside, letting me pass him to head back to my seat. I glance at the empty leather chair beside Ashton, and while I consider stealing Rhys's seat, I instead opt to sit by Ashton.

My bodyguard whispers to me as he walks back to his seat, "Your funeral."

Rhy appears surprised I chose to sit beside Ashton.

We have history, and deep down, as much as I'm angry with Ashton for wanting this life, I still have feelings for him.

Dare I admit, I'm still in love with him.

TEN

DANTE

I'm drowning, unable to come up for air, knowing my second, Moreno, is at death's door. I want to be at his side, assure Paige that the doctors are doing everything in their power to save him, but my place is as leader.

Commanding my men.

The problem is, I still don't know who I can trust.

I interrogated Matteo, who showed loyalty only to me, but that doesn't prove he isn't also loyal to the DeLuca family.

I could break knuckles, make a man bleed, but then he'd only tell me what I want to hear. Strapping him down and running a current of electricity through a man makes one talk, but all I get is babbling.

Matteo only has proven himself to work for me.

He didn't so much as sweat at my interrogation. Like he either knew how to beat it or had nothing to fear. The problem is, which is the correct answer?

My methods are sound.

I've terrorized grown men, but Matteo, he is my interrogator. He knows my playbook, which makes my methods problematic. He's not scared because he knows what he's capable of enduring.

And he's hiding *something*.

I can feel it like an itch under my skin that won't go away, but he swears he hasn't spoken to the DeLucas and had no idea of Nico's involvement.

There's not so much as a drop of sweat beading his forehead.

He's calm.

Too calm, if you ask me.

Does he show no fear because he's loyal, or because he doesn't fear me?

I can't tell.

I've either grown weak or everything that's happened is clouding my judgment. And the last thing I need is for my men to recognize weakness for what it is and threaten my throne or my family.

Lifting the barrel of the gun, I see no other choice and pull the trigger.

He's hiding something, and that's enough of a guilty verdict for me today.

The men I know I can trust are limited to one hand: Moreno, who is fighting for his life, Rhys, who is guarding Nova, Luca, and Ashton.

Liam and Sophia may soon be added to that list, but it's far too short when I have dozens of men on my payroll.

Cleaning house is in order.

I do trust Halsey enough to give him a security detail on Paige and keep an eye and update me on Moreno's condition. But he has to stay with the family; I can't let him leave.

"Sir." Bruno approaches me, albeit reluctantly. We've already had our little interrogation. He confessed that he should have known what Nico was up to, always texting on his phone, hidden in the corners in the dark on strange phone calls.

He hadn't wanted to see it for what it was.

That makes two of us.

I keep a watchful eye with Bruno, but he doesn't strike me as lying or hiding the truth.

Perhaps killing Matteo may not have been entirely in vain.

"Yes, Bruno." I give him my full attention as he comes barreling into my office.

"The McKennas are here to speak with you."

"Who?" My gaze tightens as I recognize the name, but I'm not sure why *they'd* be showing up at my front door.

"Jack and Catrina. They're worried because they haven't heard from their daughter."

"For fuck's sake," I grumble and toss my head back. "Bring them in."

Catrina rushes into my office, worry mounting on her face. Jack just looks like he's shitting bricks with his stoic expression.

"Where the hell is my daughter?" Catrina's eyes are wide, her breath stolen from her lungs and I haven't even told her the truth.

I can't tell her all of it.

I'm not even sure I should tell her *some* of it.

"She's not here," I say but force a smile. "If you'd like to see Zeke, he's in the playroom." At least he's oblivious to the turmoil happening under my roof.

Lucky bastard.

"I called my daughter and some strange man answered the phone, yelled at me, and then told me to go fuck myself!" Her eyes tear and she covers her mouth with her hand. "I didn't want to believe it was your son—and then I called him, definitely not the same voice..." Her words trail off.

Jack clears his throat, getting right to the point. “Who has our daughter?”

Catrina wipes away the stray tear. “I heard Harper pleading in the background—something is terribly wrong.”

I bite down on my tongue.

“Say something!” Catrina shouts at me, and I swallow the lump in my throat.

“Your daughter has been kidnapped.”

Catrina gasps. “What?” Her eyes are wide as she glances at her husband and clutches his arm, clinging to him. “What do you mean, kidnapped?”

“She was taken against her will. My cousin, Moreno, was shot in the head—I can’t get into the specifics.”

“Have you contacted the police? The F.B.I.?” Jack asks, stepping closer. “If our daughter is missing, why isn’t it on every news report? Why aren’t you trying to bring her home?”

ELEVEN

HARPER

My eyes lazily flutter open. There's a pounding in the front of my skull, a dense throbbing that doesn't want to cease in the slightest.

I feel sick.

I roll over on the hard floor and vomit on the cement.

My vision is foggy, my memories slowly coming back, waging war on my mind.

I've been drugged.

The ground is cold, the room dimly lit save for the light seeping in through the dirty windows above.

The place looks like a warehouse of sorts, the ceiling tall, the structure wide.

Around my neck is a collar, thick but not overly heavy, and my fingers reach around the smooth contraption, trying to find a clasp. There's no way to unbuckle or unlock the device attached to me.

Shit.

There are metal shackles on my ankles that give me several feet of movement. The chains are embedded into the cement with rusty bolts, and my fingers diligently work to loosen them, but they don't budge.

I curse under my breath. "Hello?" I shout, my throat raw, but the sound echoes throughout the large expanse and a shiver tingles along my spine.

Where am I?

My phone has long since been abandoned. I don't know when I lost the call with Luca. But when my phone buzzed and my mother called, Nico pulled the vehicle over, dug the phone out from under the seat, and blasted her for calling.

How dare she ask for me?

Inwardly, I laugh and wipe away the stray tear that slides down my cheek.

Why did she have to reach out to me today?

Or perhaps it was yesterday.

The sun is out now, and she had called when it was late, night time. I hadn't spoken with her in months and *now* she calls me, for what reason?

Certainly not fate.

Her phone call led to Nico shoving a bottle of who the hell knows what down my throat. The orange liquid in his water bottle evidently something sinister.

It couldn't just be "flavor enhancer".

No. Nico drugged me.

Within seconds of being forced to swallow that concoction, I was out cold.

Metal groans as sunlight pours into the warehouse, and I wince, trying to see who is stalking toward me.

She's no one I recognize.

"Where's Nico?" I ask, not that I want him coming for me, but at least I know the devil I'm dealing with.

Long, dark hair frames soulless eyes glancing me up and down as she saunters closer, "Would you rather deal with him?"

Wordlessly, I shake my head.

"I didn't think so, Harper."

She knows my name. I shouldn't be surprised, but I grimace at the way she says it, with such callousness and conviction. She hates me, and I'm not even sure what I did to piss her off.

My hands reach for the collar, tugging, but it doesn't budge on its own. "Take this thing off of me!" I demand, glaring up at her.

A dark smile crosses her face. "I think it looks rather *good* on you," she says with a wry smile, and my stomach churns.

"Who are you?"

She tilts her head, her face almost perfect to the extent I can't help but wonder if she's had work done, because a woman like her shouldn't be in a business like this.

She's too beautiful.

Too stunning to be doing such decrepit and dirty work, in the business of kidnapping people.

"You don't know? You murdered my husband, Santino," she says. "Livia DeLuca. I run the family empire, and you, my dear, are my new prize."

Her *prize*? What the fuck is this woman droning on about?

She retrieves a metal key from her pocket and tosses it at me. "Unchain yourself. We have work to do."

I don't dally, grabbing the key from the cold cement and unlocking the binds around my ankles. I move to stand, my legs weak and my stomach roiling at the mere decision to stand.

"Don't you dare get sick on my Louis Vuittons." Livia scowls at me.

I swallow back the bile as I slowly rise to my feet, careful not to sway or falter. The room spins and it takes everything in my power not to stumble as my vision blurs. "What do you want with me?" I ask.

Livia smiles and laughs, sliding an arm sharply between mine, like we're old friends. But there's something much more sinister about her. I can feel the fiery gates of hell opening up around us as she touches me.

"Just do as you're told and you'll be out of here shortly." Livia escorts me out of the abandoned warehouse and across the road, toward a mansion fifty yards away. Aside from the strange estate sitting on the property, there's nothing in the vicinity for miles.

The air is cold, the sun nearly cast straight overhead. It's noon or thereabouts. How long was I unconscious, a day?

I don't think.

I run.

I take off in seconds, fleeing away from the warehouse and the building a short distance ahead. There are miles of nothing on the open road, flat desert as far as the eye can see. But there has to be a road, a highway, something, *somewhere* I can get help.

The pain radiates through my neck like lightning and fire burning me, dropping me instantly to my knees in agony.

My hands grip the collar, desperate to rip it off, but it doesn't budge.

The pain extends far beyond the collar, the burning tingling down my neck, my arms, making my vision darken as I tremble for air, the throbbing unbearable, unlike anything I've ever experienced.

Livia laughs and the collar goes still.

Silent.

Tears fall aimlessly to the ground, and I slowly turn my head as I gasp for breath. My heart pounds cruelly, like it might explode after that little bit of torture.

And that smile tells me there's plenty more where that came from.

There's no bitterness in Livia's voice, no disappointment, either. "That was fun, wasn't it?" Clearly, she gets off on hurting others. "Now, get up and do as you're told."

I rise to my feet, my knees wobbly and stomach doing somersaults.

Livia points to the mansion. "Let's go."

The building is stunning: a beige stucco exterior, two stories, but it's unlike anything I've seen. There are columns extending along the veranda, keeping the harsh sun out while giving the home a Mediterranean feel.

No doubt the inside is just as luxurious as the outside.

It makes Dante's compound look like a shack, and his place is gorgeous.

There's a freshly manicured lawn, which looks out of place against the dry desert landscape around the property.

The driveway in front is brick, wide enough for multiple cars to park, but there are no visible vehicles, each of them tucked into the private garages attached to the house.

"Come inside." Livia opens the front door. She doesn't so much as use a key; it's unlocked.

With the collar attached to my neck there's no reason to lock the doors. Leaving is a death sentence.

TWELVE

BRISTOL

I can't believe Liam jetted on a plane with his sister and the rest of his housemates, leaving my ass behind.

Jerk!

Yes, I'm worried about Harper, but knowing she's missing and then being shoved aside isn't fair. I want to help.

I've been texting Liam constantly, trying to get him to spill as much information as possible. There isn't much he's willing to tell me. Which sucks.

I grab the bus, but I'm not heading back to Great Falls.

I hope I'm not making a huge mistake.

As the bus pulls up at the Breckenridge bus terminal, I climb down the steps and outside. I text my mom, hoping she's not too busy.

Can you pick me up from the bus stop in town?

Within seconds, she's calling me.

"Of course, why didn't you just call me? I'd have picked you up from school."

I pause for a beat. "Because I've been staying with Liam. I didn't think you'd want to drive down to Evergreen University."

I shiver and pull my coat closed, zipping it up. "Can you just come get me?"

"I'm heading to the car now," Mom says.

Within fifteen minutes, she's pulling up and I hurry to the car as she unlocks it. I toss my bag into the backseat and then climb up front. The warm blast of heat inside the car feels good on my frosty fingers and toes.

"Thanks for picking me up," I say, shoving my hands in front of the vents, enjoying the warm air. "Can we stop by your office?"

"We can," Mom says and glances at me briefly while mainly keeping her attention on the road. "What's going on, Bristol?"

She always cuts right to the point, and I bite down on my bottom lip, glancing at her. "Promise me you won't be mad, but I need your help."

She exhales and nods. "I promise. Just out with it."

I open my mouth and then quickly shut it. "Can I wait until Jaxson is around? I'd rather only do this once."

Mom raises an eyebrow and nods. "Good thing we're only a few minutes out."

We arrive in record time, and I leave my bag in the car and hurry into the building, Mom trailing behind me. I don't bother knocking as I trample right into Jaxson's office. "I need to talk with you."

"Bristol!" Mom scolds as I hear her click the front door shut and her heels tapping over the floorboards on her approach.

She shuts Jaxson's door behind us, assuming that whatever I intend to say may require privacy.

She's not far off the mark on that one.

"To what do I owe the pleasure, Bristol?" Jaxson leans back in his chair, staring at me. He glances briefly at my mother and I'm not quite sure, but the look they're exchanging makes me uncomfortable.

"Mom, you should take a seat for this," I say and gesture to the chair across from Jaxson's desk.

"You heard her, Emerson," Jaxson says and nods toward the empty chair for my mom to sit.

She obliges, and while there are two chairs, one still untouched, I can't sit still.

"Harper Ricci is missing," I say, the words sputtering out before I can control them. "I'm not sure if you know who that is—she's one of my boyfriend's housemates. Harper is married to Luca Ricci, the son of Dante Ricci. Mafia."

Mom and Jaxson exchange a terse glance.

"What makes you certain he's mafia?" Jaxson asks, his question careful not to reveal anything that he may or may not know.

"It slipped out. I wasn't supposed to know, but that's not the problem. The issue is that Harper has been abducted. She went missing from work—"

"We know. She should be back by now," Jaxson says, his hands clasped together, his gaze on me.

"What do you mean—you know?" I step forward, approaching his desk from the side.

He presses his lips together, quiet for only a fraction of a second. "It's come to my attention that she disappeared from her job at the Bloody Rogue." His expression is grim, and he's careful with his wording, perhaps hiding something?

"Yes, and—"

"And she was released, last seen at the Blue Sky Resort."

"She's not there now!" I pinch the bridge of my nose. "Liam isn't telling me much, but that he took a flight to Las Vegas. I can't just sit around waiting. We need to find Harper."

Jaxson and Mom exchange a quick glance between one another. "Do you know where in Vegas they're going?"

"No," I say. Liam wouldn't tell me much. "I'm worried about Harper. Please, is there anything you can do?"

Jaxson runs a hand through his dark hair and tips his head back, glancing up briefly at the ceiling. A sigh spills past his lips as he straightens his shoulders, and his attention is back on me.

"You're asking me to get involved with the mafia?" Jaxson asks.

I open my mouth and shut it.

Shit.

I glance from Jaxson to my mom, hoping she'll plead my case if he won't listen to me. "I'm asking you to help find a missing person. Harper didn't just wander away. Something happened to her."

Jaxson drums the desk with his fingers, tapping anxiously with vigor. He nods briefly. "Yeah, I'll look into it."

"Look into it?"

That's not good enough.

"I need your help. If it's payment, I'll pay whatever is

required, Jaxson. I'll volunteer every summer for the rest of my life."

His eyes crinkle. "It's not exactly volunteering if a debt is owed—but I'll see what I can find out. Why don't you go back to your desk where you used to intern, and I'll start making some phone calls."

THIRTEEN

JAXSON

I swore I wouldn't get involved with the Ricci family again.

It wasn't bad enough I had to clean up the mess they made, well, at the very least, were involved in. I don't believe Dante was caught up in trafficking women and children.

He does a lot of illegal shit around town, but he's always kept under the radar. Besides, hurting children, women, that isn't what he does. He's more of a protection mafia from what I've seen and heard: pay up or else.

I wouldn't be surprised if he runs weapons or drugs through town, and I'm sure he takes bets. I've kept my nose clean of whatever Dante involves himself with, to the point that I won't even go snooping.

I value my family, my business, and my reputation.

Dialing Dante is easy.

Talking to him, that's a hell of a lot harder.

We're both businessmen.

We protect the people we care about in different manners.

He uses brutality to get his point across.

I'd like to think that I don't have to do that, unless it's absolutely necessary.

"To what do I owe the pleasure?" Dante asks as he answers the call, recognizing my number. "I'm rather busy."

I keep the phone on speaker but gesture for Emerson to remain silent, holding a finger to my lips. I want her expertise, but Dante doesn't trust easily.

Emerson silently nods, listening to the call.

"Can't say I'm surprised. I heard your daughter-in-law is missing."

Silence ensues and I hope that I haven't spooked him.

He gives a huff, or maybe it's a sigh. The man is clearly not pleased by my knowledge of his missing in-law.

"It does seem to be a problem. One I was going to reach out to you about."

This time, I'm the one taken aback by his comment. "Is that so?" I imagine he's stroking his jaw, his eyes narrow, his gaze tight. If he were staring at me, the weight of the world through that cunning look and the desperation hidden deep within him would show.

"Harper was abducted yesterday evening while working her shift at my bar." Dante sighs and I wait, letting him continue to give me the full story. I choose not to let him know how I knew to call.

Dante continues, "She managed to escape, who I can only assume were DeLuca's men, and when I sent Nico and Moreno to retrieve her, imagine my surprise to discover my own man betrayed me."

"That's—unfortunate," I say, letting the words hang in the air as I stare at Emerson.

"Damn right it is! It's outright criminal," Dante barks and huffs under his breath.

I'm relieved that her disappearance from the bar isn't being linked back to my daughter, to Jayden, or to myself.

"I've got other problems here," Dante says, "and believe it or not, I'm calling in that favor."

I let out an obnoxious laugh. "You already called it in. I don't owe you anything—" I want this conversation over before Emerson starts asking questions. Letting her eavesdrop might have been a bad idea.

"We're not done! I helped you out of a—predicament." Dante is always careful over the phone with his words. Even in person when we've spoken, he's cautious. The man must live assuming everyone is out to get him. "Besides, how did you know Harper was missing?"

"Your son's teammate, Liam, he's dating my colleague's daughter. It's a small world," I remark with ease and a knowing grin.

He huffs, unpleased. "What does the girl know?"

I glance at Emerson, whose eyes are like two saucers. She wants to protect her daughter, I get that, but we also need to make it seem like we're on the same side. "Not much. Came here concerned about a friend missing from work. I told her I thought it was nothing, especially since it hasn't been on the news—"

Dante interrupts me. "Liam's girlfriend," he repeats, and I can't tell if he's making a mental note or jotting the information down for later. "The girl have a name?"

"Not mine to give, but I'm sure you can figure it out." I smirk and lean back in my leather desk chair.

"Fine. Fine. That can wait." Dante gets right back to the point. "I've got resources indicating that the DeLucas have several properties in and around the Las Vegas area. Can you look a little deeper for me? I suspect they're putting her up in some place remote, likely where there'd be an auction."

"An auction?" I repeat, making sure I hear him correctly. "Are you telling me the DeLucas are still alive?" I run a hand through my unkempt hair and exhale heavily.

I thought he'd stopped the DeLucas and ended things with their human trafficking ring for good. I'd helped clean up the mess. He assured me that it was over. The last thing I need is a target on my back because they are still operating.

Anger flows through me along with annoyance. "My sources told me they were finished. You assured me they were put out of business!" I snap at Dante, pushing back my chair and standing, pacing the office, the heat licking my skin as I can't help dread the thought of anything happening to my family, my wife, my children.

"Massimo and his son, Santino, are deceased. It seems his wife is running the business, giving orders, and is wholly responsible for Harper's abduction. I need every residence, property, business that she owns in Nevada."

That's an easy request, given the type of work that I do for a living. I plant my ass back at my desk and type away at the keyboard.

"She has nothing registered to her, but there are several shell corporations that I know for a fact DeLuca ran. Let me dig a little deeper—" I keep typing away, trying to pull up data where it's not so easy to check.

We run background checks, credit reports, drug tests, the type of requests made by employers prior to hiring a new employee.

"Anything?" Dante asks tersely, a bit impatient as I type as quickly as I can, trying to dig up information for him.

"There's a property in Las Vegas, on the outskirts of town. Let me pull up satellite footage and see what it looks like." I tap away at the keyboard, putting in data, waiting for it to load.

I zoom in, surveying the data. "Wow. Yeah, there's a nice estate in the middle of nowhere. Looks like it has some kind of storage hanger or warehouse on the property. Could hold an airplane, I'm not sure."

"Give me the address."

I gather the details and give it to Dante. "You know I can't just sit on the information, knowing a girl has been abducted."

"I'm already on it, I have a team ready, we just need a plane..." his voice trails off. "And I could use your help for other matters as well..."

I glance up at Emerson, who has been silently listening to the call on speakerphone.

She grabs my notepad on the desk and scribbles something down.

Her expertise right now is incredibly valuable. "We have a plane in Breckenridge. What else?" I ask.

Asking me two favors, that means shit is really bad for Dante if he's still asking for help. He doesn't cozy up to me unless it's life or death.

"Harper's parents are demanding custody of Zeke, and they're going to the police to file a missing person's report. There's only so much that I can do..."

"Isn't *your man* the chief of police?" He's as dirty as they come.

"Yes, but I don't own the local news stations, and if the McKennas reach out to them—"

"I'll see what I can do."

FOURTEEN

HARPER

Livia's tight-lipped smile is entirely her scheming. I'm just unsure what she's up to. Bringing me here, into her mansion, the collar around my neck, I need to figure a way out of this—alive.

"Don't take this the wrong way, but you stink."

"Being drugged and thrown into a warehouse will do that to a person," I snap.

She laughs under her breath and escorts me through the mansion on the main floor, down the hallway and to a closed door.

Livia opens it, flips on the light.

It's a bathroom.

"Do us both a favor and get cleaned up."

"You brought me here to shower?" I don't buy it. I stare at her skeptically, and she slides her hand into her pocket.

"We can do this the easy way or the hard way."

A jolt of electricity blinds me, rippling in waves through my neck, bringing me down to my knees.

It only lasts a fraction of a second.

A warning.

Unlike the last time when I ran, she was quick with the pulse, the pain.

Gasping for breath, my heart races, and I stare up at her, the devil. I grind my teeth, snarling, "Fucking bitch."

Livia laughs and tilts her head. "You're just now figuring that out? Well done, Harper. Get in the shower. Don't make me ask you again."

My fingers graze the necklace.

Water and electricity don't mix.

"What about—" I finger the collar, tapping on the exterior.

Will she remove it?

"Don't piss me off and you'll be fine."

She pushes me into the bathroom and shuts the door behind me.

There's no lock, anyone can enter on a whim.

Great.

There's a glass shower door and I open it, reaching for the faucet, turning the handle on and to hot, making the water the right temperature.

The bathroom is an interior room. There are no windows, no way to escape from inside.

I turn on the fan and then slowly open the main door, hoping I might be able to sneak out.

Livia glances up from her phone, raising an eyebrow at me.

"What about clean clothes and a towel?" I ask, doing my best not to seem like I'm up to trouble. I was hoping I might escape, but she's standing there guarding the door like a hellhound.

"There are fresh linens in the bath closet." She pushes past me into the bathroom, and to the left, there's a small closet filled with towels and washcloths. A small chute sits on the interior wall inside the closet. "Toss your dirty clothes and towels down the laundry chute."

Livia shoves me back into the bathroom.

So much for sneaking out unnoticed.

Even if I manage to escape with the collar on, how far would I get before she realizes I'm gone and jolt me?

How much distance do I need until her remote is disabled? Feet? Miles?

I don't look at my reflection in the mirror. The bathroom has steamed, leaving a fog over the glass. Bending down, I open the cabinets under the sink.

Empty.

Perhaps if I break the mirror, I could use a shard as a weapon to get away.

There's nothing to break it with, except my fist and a towel. Even the shampoo and conditioner containers are affixed to the shower wall, bolted in place.

Well, fuck.

I step into the shower, staring down at the dirty water curling around my feet. My shoulders are tense, my head throbs and the hot water dulls the ache for a few moments.

The shower is peaceful, tranquil.

I imagine it's the last bit of peace and quiet that I might have.

The bathroom door breezes open. "Time's up," Livia commands, and the cold air rushes into the shower. I turn off the tap, having had barely enough time to fully cleanse every inch of me from head to toe.

Opening the glass door, Livia tosses the fluffy white towel at me, but not before giving me a once-over with her eyes.

"And what about clothes?"

She grabs my filthy ensemble that I wore to the bar and shoves it down the laundry chute. There isn't enough space for a person to fit, I already checked.

"Come with me."

I secure the towel around my chest, gripping it in the front with my hand.

My hair drips down my shoulders and back. The marble floor cold against my feet as I leave a trail of wet footprints in the hallway.

I obediently follow Livia, if only for the mere fact that I'm wearing that stupid collar and I don't want another bolt of electricity coursing through me.

Not now.

Not ever.

Is that what it feels like to be tased?

"Where are you taking me?" I follow behind her across the hallway. She leads me to a room, it appears to be a bedroom, and opens the door, gesturing for me to step foot inside.

"There is a paper gown for you to put on. Our in-house physician will be with you shortly."

"What?" My eyes widen in horror. "Absolutely not!"

"Do you think you get a choice?" she asks, staring at me pointedly. "We have to make sure that our girls are clean before being brought downstairs."

Clean.

"I already showered."

What the hell is she talking about?

Doctor. Clean.

I'm going to be sick.

It's no secret that her husband trafficked women and children. "You want to test me for STIs." It's a logical guess and she smirks, tilting her head.

"Smart girl. We can't have our clientele catching something from one of our girls."

She reaches for my hair, fingering a strand. "Such a pretty young thing. It's a shame you're not a virgin. You'd have gone for a lot more than a married whore."

I spit in her face, glaring at her.

She rips the towel from my clutches, her gaze inspecting my body as she circles me like a vulture. "It's a pity you have stretch marks." Livia's fingers graze my skin, and I flinch from her touch.

"Do not touch me!" I seethe, snarling at her.

The smile never leaves her face. She's not the least bit afraid of me, because she's in complete control. "Or what, dear? You'll scream. Good, many of my men like screamers. Remember that when they buy your time."

"I'm not for sale." My gaze moves over and across the room; there are no windows, no exits except for the door. The room doesn't appear like a doctor's office. There's no medical bed or supplies in sight.

Instead, there's a plush queen-sized mattress against the wall, a dresser and a desk lined opposite, and a door that, I assume, leads to a closet.

In the corner of the room near the ceiling, is a camera with a red light, indicating we're being watched, likely by her security team.

Even if I could flee, there's still the matter of the electronic device around my neck. At the very least, she'll torture me if I attempt an escape, but is that worse than what I'll be forced to endure if I stay?

Livia comes to stand behind me, nudging me into the room, her hand on my back, forcing me to enter.

"Given your behavior," Livia says and stalks past me toward the bed where a paper gown is folded, she snatches it up. "Perhaps you'll learn to show some respect." She takes the gown with her along with my towel, leaving me naked as she slams the door shut.

"Wait!" I scream, pounding on the closed wooden door. The handle doesn't so much as budge as I try to yank it open.

I'm locked inside.

FIFTEEN

LUCA

"You're telling me she's in there?" I nod toward the towering building in the distance.

"That's what Dante's intel is telling us. Her phone is off," Ashton says, giving me a look of pity.

I don't need his pity.

We have a trunkload of equipment. Sophia inspects the small drone that's sitting on the ground. There's a remote control, and she fiddles with it, getting the drone up a few feet off the ground but then sets it carefully back down.

She's practicing, but for what? I don't see how the drone is going to be of much use.

We need to get Harper out, now.

I cling to the belief that Livia DeLuca wouldn't kill my wife. She may want revenge, but a mafia boss doesn't get their hands dirty.

I glare at Sophia, annoyed by the drone that she's playing with. Now isn't the time to be screwing around.

"Careful," Liam warns his sister as he glances through the equipment in the back of the SUV, finding a micro camera and turning it on. The feed links to a tablet. "We don't want anyone to notice we're here."

I don't do well sitting still, waiting to rescue my wife.

I pace outside, anxiety prickling at my skin, my stomach in knots.

"We need video, *now*." I glare at Rhys, who is working diligently to gain us access to surveillance cameras. He's pulling up satellite internet on the laptop; it's a multi-step process and I don't want to stand around and wait.

"Patience, Luca. I'm working as fast as I can, believe me, I want justice as much as you do."

"Vengeance," I seethe, glaring at him. "They took *my wife*. They threatened *my son*."

The DeLucas won't stop until they're all dead.

Liam stalks over toward us, leaving Sophia to manage the drone on her own. "How's the footage from inside the compound coming?"

"I just got the link from Dante's source. As soon as I log in with the parameters, we'll have full access to every camera inside and outside the property."

Rhys types away at the keyboard, clicking hastily, and manages within a few short seconds to pull up footage. There are more than a dozen cameras, and it takes some sorting and rearranging the feed on his screen to find Harper.

She's naked, the footage grainy, but the anger bubbles in my veins.

"What the fuck are they doing to her?" I growl, stepping closer, examining the video, and Rhys turns the sound up.

The door opens, a gentleman steps inside, shutting the door behind himself.

"Who is that?" Sophia asks, setting the drone back down on the ground. She places the remote inside the trunk of the vehicle, glancing at the footage with us.

"Turn up the volume," I say, giving Rhys orders, even though he's the one with the most experience, practically running the show.

"I'm Dr. Barone, I'm here to give you your physical examination and run some quick swabs and a blood test to make sure you're clean."

"The hell you are," Harper snaps, quickly moving out of his reach.

"I was informed you were a troublesome one. Shall I bring in the guards to hold you down while we perform our examination?" The doctor stalks closer, and I shake my head in disgust.

"Don't you dare fucking touch her!" I growl, momentarily forgetting that the doctor can't hear me. "What are we waiting for?"

Why isn't the team strapping on weapons and ammunition?

"I'm pregnant." Harper's voice makes my heart thud uncontrollably.

I shake my head. "No."

It can't be true.

We've been careful—and she would have told me. But then again, we haven't had time alone together the past couple of days, between the hockey game, her new job, thanks to my father...

"I'm not leaving my pregnant wife fending for herself!"

Fuck it all.

I stalk clear across the desert, leaving our vehicle and carrying a pistol at my hip and a rifle strapped across my back.

We'll need more ammunition if Livia DeLuca has the place fortified, but my goal is getting Harper back. The rest, the team can figure out.

Ashton races after me and grabs my arm. "You can't just walk up and ring the doorbell."

I snort. "You think I'm just going to waltz up and wait for that monster to shoot me? I'm going in guns blazing. No one goes after *my wife and unborn child.*"

Rhys eyes me up and down, gesturing for me to come back to the vehicle. "Ashton is right. That's nowhere near enough ammo, and we don't know what we're walking into. It'll be an ambush."

I want him to be wrong, but Livia is holding Harper hostage. The new mafia boss must realize we're coming. She'd be a fool not to expect us.

"At least go in smart, fully loaded, with audio and video. We can map out a blueprint with the right tools," Liam says and digs through the open trunk, pulling out surveillance tech that was sent to us through one of Dante's contacts. We had a package along with weapons waiting at the airport hangar upon our arrival.

Liam hands me a camera that is the size of a button and clips it to my shirt. They'll have eyes inside, audio too.

"Come on, they're going to expect me to be wired," I say.

Liam makes sure the button looks ordinary and doesn't appear out of place on my shirt. "Do you plan on getting caught?"

I huff under my breath.

"No one plans on getting caught," I mutter.

"Good. Then get us intel that we can use. We need a map of the facility."

They're fucking using me as bait. I glare at Liam, not the least bit surprised or pleased, but I'm not about to wait for more information from Dante's sources. There's not enough time in the world for that. Harper's life is on the line. Along with her dignity.

Fuck that doctor wanting to examine her.

Touch her.

I'm the only man allowed to touch my wife *like that*.

I chance a quick glance at the screen and grimace.

Harper is lying on a bed, the doctor touching her, and God help me, I want to cut his balls off.

I will castrate the bastard who lays a finger on *my wife*.

"Get us good footage, and we'll be in within minutes. We just need to know where you're both being held and how many we're up against."

I pause, staring at the mansion in front of us. There's no gate, it's easily accessible, but quite remote. Mountains surround us as we're at the bottom of a valley.

I can't just stare at the damn compound and not do something. Restlessness pricks under my skin. Waiting is a ticking time bomb, and Harper might not be alive if I waste another second.

"This is a terrible plan. You're just going to give Livia what she wants?" Ashton asks.

"Actually, I am." I remove the rifle, shoving it into his hands. "See you on the other side."

"What the fuck are you doing?" Rhys grinds his teeth and chases after me, but I'm already out of earshot.

"I'm going to save my wife and child!" I shout back at him.

While they bicker about the best way into the mansion, I'm doing exactly what no one would expect: walking up to the front door.

Why?

Because I can't protect Harper if I'm not with her.

"Fucking Luca," Rhys curses, and I'm sure they'll come up with a plan to get both of us out. If not, it'll be up to me to save us both. But at least I'll have given them eyes on the inside.

As I approach the property, I survey the windows, the balcony, and roof. There are no sharpshooters, no one aiming a gun at me. There are, however, cameras at every juncture, and I feel watchful eyes on me as I walk up to the front door and let myself inside.

Time to fuck things up for the DeLucas.

SIXTEEN

HARPER

The examination by that atrocious doctor makes me shudder.

Thankfully, it's over, and the moment he stalks out of the room, Livia returns.

"Just great," I mutter. If it's not one hell, it's another.

She tosses me a pair of gray, scratchy sweats and a matching shirt. It feels like prison clothes.

"Put these on."

I do as she commands, only because I'm naked and I don't want to be paraded around and humiliated.

"Congratulations are in order," Livia says, smirking as she watches me dress.

The moment my clothes are donned, she grabs my arm and escorts me through the halls.

I only give her a look of confusion because I don't know what she's congratulating me on. I'm not actually pregnant.

I can't be.

I mean, I don't think it's possible—but I haven't had my *friend* come to visit yet this month.

My mind ticks over the days of the month, trying to remember when my last period was.

Oh fuck.

"You're pregnant. We ran a quick test; turns out you weren't lying. Imagine my surprise and delight. While I'd usually put the newborn on the open market when they're born, your little one is extra special to me."

The nausea falls over me like waves crashing toward the shoreline. Sweat trickles my brow, and I stumble slightly.

Livia is right at my side, her hand on my arm, dragging me along with her. "The little one you're carrying has DeLuca bloodlines. Seeing as how you murdered my husband, you owe me that child."

"I don't owe you anything," I snarl at her.

"You do, but we have time for that—you're only a few weeks pregnant."

There's no way she's taking my baby. She's fucking crazy.

"Now, now, don't be so upset. It'll be our little secret for tonight."

She winks at me, and I taste bile in my mouth, swallowing my disgust.

"Come, let me take you to the others."

While I haven't seen too many guards when entering the mansion, there are many more up ahead. She leads me farther inside the mansion, toward a set of wrought iron doors on the first floor, intricate and locked.

The guard nearest the door unlocks the gate entrance, and Livia gestures for me to enter.

A wave of dizziness washes over me, and I press my lips together, hiding the discomfort. The last thing I want is to appear weak to the monster keeping me locked up.

Regret fills me. I should have fought harder against that stupid doctor or Livia upstairs, when there weren't other guards around. I may have been able to escape.

Once I step past those locked gates, there's no exiting on my own.

"Walk!" Livia commands and reaches into her pocket for that stupid remote control to torture me.

I step forward, if only because I'd rather be trapped than experience another jolt of electricity around my neck.

That's the reason I can't fight.

Every time I attempt to challenge Livia or anyone of power here, I'm subdued. And the pain is atrocious, unlike anything I've ever experienced.

My breathing is shallow and my heart quickens as she brushes past me, leading me down the hallway.

From behind, I hear the firm metal clasp of the gate.

Whatever awaits me is sure to be the depths of hell.

"What do you want from me?" I ask, obediently following her farther inside. There are guards in the hallway, men armed with guns and daggers attached to their clothes. Of the five guards I count, only the ones on the other side of the gate are wearing protective armor.

These men are in shirts and pants, armed for a war with whom exactly?

Livia opens the door to the left and nods for me to enter. "Go." She shoves me when I don't move quickly enough.

The room is dimly lit, the floor a cold marble with an oversized area rug in the center.

She slams the door shut behind me and I glance at the other young women my ages or even possibly younger.

I inhale sharply, my hands in front of me, wringing them together. Anxiety pricks at my skin, my stomach heavy like lead.

A girl, maybe all of fourteen or fifteen, hurries over to me now that I'm locked inside.

"I'm Margaret."

"Harper." I give her my name and she takes my arm, leading me toward where with the other girls are sitting on the floor.

There's a bench along the wall and a handful of blankets shoved into makeshift beds.

"How long have you been here?" I ask, my voice quiet, afraid that the guards or Livia might barge in on a whim.

There are two cameras in the room, the obnoxious red light indicating that we're being watched.

"I'm not sure. Months," she says. "It gets easier." She leads me to sit on one of the blankets.

"I don't plan on sticking around for long," I say.

Margaret takes a seat on the blanket, her legs at her side, waiting for me to join her.

My gaze peruses the room. There are no windows, only one door in which I entered. There are multiple guards out in the hallway and a locked gate that we'll have to get through in order to escape.

It won't be easy.

Damn near impossible.

My silence has her staring at me.

"Yeah, I thought the same thing. But every time you fight—" She taps the collar around her neck, the same one that is fastened and jolted electricity through me.

I glance at her bright round eyes. They're nearly steel-colored, and her skin pale and freckled. Her hair a mess of red curls, tangled and unkempt.

"Has no one escaped?" I ask, chancing a glance at the cameras.

"Don't worry, no audio." She pats the blanket for me to sit.

I oblige if only to appease her, desperate for answers.

Margaret leans closer, whispering to me, "Some of the girls leave, but they always come back."

"How long?"

I ask, assuming she means the time spent with a buyer, perhaps a couple of hours. Has no one tried escaping then?

"They keep us here for us to breed. We'll be auctioned off for an hour or two, forced to do whatever the buyer desires. The highest bidder is always first. They tend to sneak in alcohol, pills, a way to help us relax. We are shuffled from one buyer to the next until the early hours of the night," she whispers. "Then we're thrown back in here with the other girls until the next auction."

My mouth goes dry and I wipe my sweaty hands on my black pants. I want Margaret to be wrong, mistaken. But the look in her eyes, she's not lying to me. There's no reason for her to trick me.

"No." I shake my head, denial the only way through this horror.

"The way out is pregnant, but it's only temporary."

The air is knocked right there out of my lungs, and my fingers grip the bedsheets. The room spins and I shut my eyes, pushing away the creeping anxiety. It's loud enough that I swear the sound of my heartbeat can be heard for miles.

"Rumor has it the Madam makes most of her money when those of us fall pregnant, auctioning off newborns like cattle. She moves any pregnant girls out of here, gives better accommodations until after the birth."

I'm going to be sick. My head falls between my legs, gasping for breath.

She rests a comforting hand on my back. "It sounds awful, but most of the men are quick."

SEVENTEEN

LUCA

No one greets me.

There are no guards at the entrance, but I suppose Dante doesn't keep guards at the front door to his compound, either.

Most people aren't stupid enough to waltz right up and enter the mafia's home.

I'm not *most people*.

If DeLuca hadn't been foolish enough to abduct my wife, I wouldn't be here.

Which means I don't need an invitation.

I take a thorough glance from left to right, making sure the camera catches every detail for them to map the interior of the property.

Who exactly did Dante team up with for this level of equipment? I've never known for him to have any type of spy or tactical gear, outside of guns, ammunitions, and maybe a bulletproof vest for safe measure.

The sound of boots carries down the hallway, and I keep moving, making sure not to be seen, at least not by whoever is coming. I can't help the cameras. Had we spent more time planning, maybe someone could have infiltrated the system.

I weave through the hallway and notice a wrought-iron door, much like a gate, inside the house. There are three guards on the opposite side.

It's unlikely there's a basement, given the soil and terrain. The metal door with a lock *inside* the property, dead giveaway.

That must be where they're keeping Harper.

Footsteps grow near, and I hide in a nearby supply closet but don't quite shut the door, waiting for the soldier to wander by. I grab my dagger from my boot and grip the handle, holding my breath.

He saunters past, and I quietly exit the closet and sneak up from behind. I slice the blade across the base of his throat.

He falls to the ground in a heap. I drag him into the hall closet, out of sight of the cameras and anyone who wanders by. There's a small splatter of crimson on the floor, smeared.

Well, I'm not exactly a pro at this shit.

I strip him down to his underwear and white t-shirt underneath, wearing his uniform, ensuring the camera is tucked hidden onto the new outfit before stealing his weaponry. The dark military ensemble is heavy, and the vest is bulletproof. I don his hat and keep my head bent down.

Attached to my ensemble is a set of keys on my belt loop. I grab the keys as I head toward the metal-gated door.

The guards don't pay me a lick of attention as I approach the lock. I'm not sure which one is the right key, but the first several look more like house keys. Just a brief examination of the lock and it resembles a skeleton style key. Thankfully, there are two of those on the keychain.

I reach for the first key and shove it into the lock, hoping it'll open.

It doesn't budge.

I keep my head down, quietly withdraw the key and try again with the second skeleton key. There's a smear of blood on my hand and I deftly wipe it on the dark slacks, hoping there isn't more blood splatter that I can't see.

The lock clicks with ease, and I open the door, stepping inside, closing it but not securing it tight.

I'll need an escape route, in case shit goes down fast.

"Make sure you slam the door," another guard echoes to me down the hallway.

I grunt and nod, grabbing the metal, forcing it to rattle, but I'm careful not to latch it.

That seems to appease him, and I take in my surroundings.

Three guards are patrolling this single hallway.

Harper must be nearby.

One guard stands outside a closed door. I walk past him as if I own the place and yank open the door.

There are dozens of girls, and all of them turn toward the now open door, staring, watching, and waiting.

I stalk into the room; it's not the room from the surveillance footage, but there are several girls being held captive.

They could have moved Harper.

I glance at each of them as I search for my wife, relieved when I find Harper sitting on a makeshift bed on the floor with another girl.

"Boss wants to have a chat with you," I say, keeping my head bent down. I grab Harper's arm, dragging her to her feet.

"Get your grimy paws off me!" she snarls, and I catch her gaze.

It flickers and flashes with hatred.

She yanks away from me like I'm the enemy, but it has to be an act.

"I'm not going anywhere with you."

"Is that so?" I ask and glance her over, gripping her arm, forcing her to follow me into the hallway.

"The collar," the guard says, like it's a reminder.

My eyes land on the device secured around her neck.

Shit.

What the hell is that thing?

"Please, no!" Harper pleads with me, and my stomach flops. The fear in her voice is real.

Does she think I'd purposefully hurt her, to make them believe I'm one of them?

"Then you'll do as I say, won't you?" I keep my hand affixed around her arm as I yank her out of the room and toward the metal gated door I left unlocked.

"Boss is that way," the guard says and points in the opposite direction.

I shove Harper behind me, shielding her with my body as I lift the barrel and shoot at the armed men as we hurry backward through the gated door.

Slamming the gate shut, forcing them to unlock it if they want to chase after us, I grab Harper's hand, pulling her in the direction of the front entrance.

Several guards approach from around the corner near the door, blocking our escape. Guns drawn, a woman steps out from behind them, a small black device in her hand. She presses the button, and Harper collapses to the ground, trembling.

Screaming.

"Stop!" I shout, commanding the woman to obey me.

Livia DeLuca.

She removes her thumb from the trigger, and Harper gasps for breath, panting hard from the floor. Her forehead is slick with sweat, her body weak after the assault.

The men surround us with guns pointed at us from every direction. I kick my weapon away, showing that I'm unarmed, and bend down, lifting Harper into my arms. "You'll let my wife go."

"I'll do no such thing," Livia says with a cunning wickedness that sends an icy chill down my spine. "Mercurio, show them to their new accommodations."

I carry Harper, it's the least I can do considering she'd just been jolted with several volts of electricity.

What else had they done to her while she was their hostage?

Her breathing is soft, raspy, her heart still pounding wildly as she trembles every so often in my arms, like her body is trying to catch up after the onslaught of violence within it.

I press a kiss to her forehead, hoping that the team will be inside soon, break through the front door and subdue the guards.

Slowly, I walk forward, following Mercurio, taking my time, giving Ashton and the others an opportunity to come rescue us.

But I can't be that lucky.

There's a gun shoved at my back, forcing me to press onward.

"Move!" the guard behind me beckons, and I pick up my pace, my arms holding Harper as we're led down the hallway, farther into the compound.

EIGHTEEN

DANTE

I pay a visit to Moreno, pleased that he's woken from his coma.

Paige has been by his bedside every waking hour. She needs rest. "Go home, shower." I glance her over; she looks rougher than Moreno does.

"I—" She stalls, and I can see the hesitation, the desire not to leave his side, worry that something might happen. I'd feel that way, too, if anything happened to my Nikki.

But he's awake.

Has been for a couple of hours. I drove my ass down to the hospital to see if there was anything new he could tell me. Anything that he might remember from that day.

But that conversation won't happen around Paige. I don't need her worrying about business matters.

Moreno smiles weakly, his voice thick. "Go home. Dante is right. Get some sleep. Actual sleep, love. In a bed."

Paige shakes her head. "Absolutely not. I'll shower and then I'll be right back." She glances down at her jeans and sweater. "I could use a fresh change of clothes too."

"Take your time, love."

Paige leans down, planting a soft kiss on Moreno's mouth, and I turn around, not needing to witness their intimate moment.

I clear my throat when she hasn't left yet and glance over my shoulder at the two of them.

"Right," Paige whispers and her fingers squeeze his hand before letting go, quietly leaving the hospital room. "I love you."

"I love you too. Now go, shower, sleep, get some rest," Moreno says, glancing her over. "That's an order."

She laughs under her breath.

That woman never takes orders from me; I can't imagine Paige takes them from Moreno, but she doesn't argue.

I wait until she's gone and feel both relief and sadness wash over me. I hate how worried she was, attentive to his needs, and had been waiting for him to wake up.

I wouldn't want Nikki to have sleepless nights at my bedside, and yet without a doubt she'd be doing the exact same thing.

"How are you feeling?" I ask, approaching his bedside.

Moreno's eyes crinkle. "Honestly? I hurt like hell."

"You were shot in the head," I remind him, wondering how much of the incident he actually remembers. The doctors warned of amnesia surrounding the event.

"That's what they say," Moreno says and shrugs, wincing. "I remember driving to go get Harper and then—nothing after. What happened? Paige wouldn't tell me specifics."

I exhale heavily. I had been here, hoping he'd be giving me information, not the other way around.

"Nico shot you and abducted Harper. Turns out, he's been working for the DeLucas all along."

Moreno rubs at his eyes, the monitors increasing in urgency with each breath he takes. His pulse and blood pressure are increasing simultaneously. "I never suspected…" he trails off, disgust filling his voice. "He was one of us!"

I rest a reassuring arm on his shoulder. "Don't blame yourself." Staring down at him, I remove my hands, sliding them into my pockets. "I interrogated the capos."

"And?"

"Matteo was hiding something." I meet his stare, and he raises an eyebrow.

I offer a curt nod, a silent understanding.

He's deceased.

"Anyone else?"

"Can't say for certain. I've brought Rhys back in; he's your daughter's new personal bodyguard."

The color drains from Moreno's face. "Nova needs a bodyguard, why exactly? Who has been threatening my daughter?"

"After Harper's disappearance, I thought it might be good to protect the family. Nova isn't mafia but like you said, she's your daughter. If the DeLucas want to hurt us..."

"Appreciated." Moreno's eyes flicker and I sense his concern.

"She's in good hands; I can assure you Rhys knows how to protect her."

"But where are Rhys and Nova now?" Moreno asks, glancing past me. She hasn't come to visit, and while I had hoped he wouldn't notice, that was unlikely and foolish.

Best to rip the Band-Aid off.

"Against better judgment and my direct orders, she boarded a plane with Luca, Ashton, and the others to go get Harper."

The monitors beep haphazardly, and a slew of nurses rush into his room to check on him.

I'm shuffled out, against Moreno's request. "Let him stay! I demand answers!" Moreno shouts, forgetting perhaps who is in charge.

He reports to me, not the other way around.

I step out into the hallway at the insistence of the hospital staff while they check his vitals and inevitably sedate him.

Paige is going to be pissed when she finds out Nova is with Rhys in Nevada. I let Paige believe her daughter was back at the compound, trying to help with Harper's disappearance. Since she hadn't been home, there had been no way for her to know otherwise.

The cell phone reception in this place is horrible. I head down to the elevator, making my way into the hospital lobby to check my phone.

There are several missed texts and calls from both Rhys and Ashton. Two more texts from Jaxson Monroe.

Not a word from my son.

How odd.

I glance at the texts, briefly read through them. It's mostly updates on the plane landing, heading to the DeLuca compound, and then my stomach drops to the ground.

It's the text from Rhys which has me calling him, wondering what the hell happened in the past couple of hours.

Luca is using himself as bait.

Why the fuck is my son the bait? Why didn't Ashton or Liam offer themselves up, and what the hell plan are they thinking?

Rhys answers on the first ring.

"Tell me Luca is safe."

"I wish I could do that, sir."

Wincing, I step outside. The air in the lobby is hot, suffocating. I need to breathe. "What the hell happened, Rhys?" My heart wants to slam outside of my chest, trying to break free from its cage.

"Luca couldn't wait for us to come up with a plan, so he ran in headfirst to rescue Harper. And it went about as well as you might expect."

I curse and shake my head, unpleased with the latest revelation. "Any chance he brought in any surveillance equipment?"

Jaxson had provided a full load of spy-grade audio and video technology at the airport hangar. I'd made sure the team had access before rescuing Harper from the DeLucas.

"He grabbed a camera and still has it on. There's audio too. I've got Sophia mapping out the house based on the video footage that's being sent."

"Good. What else?" Rhys is typically Nova's bodyguard. He's not usually running point on a mission. But he's got the most experience on the team that I sent—and heaven help me now that Luca has been captured.

"We're missing a lot of footage. We only have two hallways in the compound, and there's an entire wing we haven't laid eyes on. There are dozens of cameras inside; we need access."

"I'll have my source work on that," I say. "And Luca, how is he?"

"Alive."

NINETEEN

JAXSON

I've spent the past day making sure all security tech and weapons are transported to the hangar where Dante's team lands. I've also secured them an eight-passenger SUV and had the gear loaded into the trunk, along with a laptop. That was the least of my problems, Dante also asked me to dig into the custody situation for him.

Jack and Catrina are fighting for full-custody of Harper's son, Zeke.

How does this concern me? Dante insisted I run every background check imaginable, dig up dirt, find something on Harper's parents so that he could presumably use it for blackmail and have them drop the custody suit.

The problem is they're perfectly clean, albeit they don't have the best credit score, and their savings account is low, but it's not enough to convince a judge that they're not worthy legal guardians or to blackmail them over.

What had Dante hoped to find?

Did he suspect that Jack, who is a manager for Blue Sky Resort, was embezzling money from his job? There aren't any hefty deposits; they clearly live paycheck-to-paycheck.

My phone buzzes on my desk and I recognize the caller I.D. and grumble.

"Hey, Dante. What can I do for you?" I swear I'd love to be rid of him, but his power and influence extend far beyond Breckenridge.

"I need another favor."

I laugh under my breath. "Of course, you do. We're at three, is it now?"

"Not that anyone's counting," Dante grumbles. "The

surveillance equipment, excellent stuff. I need something a little more illegal."

Does he think the high-tech shit I gave him was legal? It dropped off the back of a government contractor's van.

"What do you need?"

"There are cameras inside DeLuca's compound. The location you gave me, spot on."

"Of course, it was," I say, not the least bit surprised by either of those comments. "Let me guess, you want access to the footage inside the compound?"

I already have Declan working on hacking the infrastructure and getting past the firewall. For him, it's just another day at the office; for me, asking him to do not only something illegal but for the Riccis, it makes me physically ill.

But he doesn't know the specifics, and he never will. One of the benefits of working for me, he'll never take the fall for the illegal shit I do for Dante. I keep my men clean and protected.

I swear I can hear the smile in Dante's voice. "Video,

audio, I want whatever there is available. We need to see where they're keeping Harper and Luca."

Pursing my lips, I'm well aware Luca is Dante's son.

"Luca is with them?" I ask, not believing what I'm hearing. I hang my head, pinching the bridge of my nose. This is going to get messy. Dante would start a war for going after Harper, but his only heir—

He'd burn the world to protect his son.

And anyone who gets in his way is dead.

The last thing I want is to stand in Dante Ricci's way when he goes to slaughter the DeLucas.

"*My son* decided to go in and save his wife."

There's a coldness to his tone, a hint of defiance, and I suspect Luca is more like Dante than both of them realize.

"I already have my best guy working on access to the footage," I say.

"Well, work faster. Harder." Dante's irritation is impossible to ignore. I don't, however, want it directed at me. "Fuck!"

I hold my breath for a fraction of a second. I don't want to ask what's wrong, but he answers before I even have time.

"Turn on the fucking television." Dante is irate, and I reach for the remote. In the corner of the room, affixed to the wall, is a television. I turn the device on, watching as the local news broadcast displays a *Breaking News* alert.

On the left side of the screen is a recent picture of Harper Ricci, her name under the photograph. On the opposite side, her parents doing a press conference, begging for her to be returned.

"Our daughter, Harper, was taken last night. She has blonde hair, dark-brown eyes. She's nineteen years old, a mother, she wouldn't have run off and left her son behind or her husband. We're offering a reward of fifty thousand dollars for the safe return of our daughter, Harper. If anyone knows or has seen anything, please come forward. Harper, if you can see this, please come home. Please know that we won't stop looking for you, Harper, searching for you. We love you, Harper. Your son, Zeke, loves you, Harper. He misses his mother."

I notice the overuse of her first name, typical in abductions, trying to humanize her, in case the perpetrator is watching the news.

There's no mention of Luca's disappearance or abduction. Are her parents unaware or strictly only concerned about Harper's well-being? And how the hell are they offering a fifty-thousand-dollar reward when their bank accounts don't have anything close to five figures, let alone six?

Except Jack McKenna has a retirement fund from Blue Sky Resort. I grab the file, glancing through the papers that I've dug up on Harper's father.

He must be planning on cashing in his retirement if they find Harper.

I mute the television, the closed-captioning popping up at the bottom of the screen. "I have to say, I'm surprised you're running this with the news stations. I would have thought you'd have wanted to keep the whole situation quiet and handle it discreetly."

There's a dark, sinister laugh that vibrates through the phone. "Do you think this was up to me? The fucking McKennas went behind my back. Not only are they going to fight for custody of Zeke, but they're also interfering in our rescue attempt. They're going to get their daughter killed!"

"The rescue attempt that involved getting your son abducted?" I quip. I should know better than to piss off a mafia boss, but sometimes I can't help myself.

"Are you going to help me or what?"

"I will get you a link to the live footage within the hour," I say.

Declan better have it hacked and accessible without anyone noticing.

"And what about the McKennas? Anything I can use to stop them from trying to take Zeke from us? I need something dark, off the books type of stuff. They threatened to file for sole custody."

He wants blackmail material.

"They're a little too squeaky clean. Not so much as a traffic violation for either one of them."

"Come on, Jaxson, you can do better than that," he says.

I know what he's asking for, but I refuse to soil my reputation or land in prison for his dirty work. "I'm not making up shit and putting it on a file for you to use at a hearing against them."

TWENTY

LUCA

The accommodations for a prison are better than one might expect. Instead of being detained in a basement like my father's holding cell, we're locked in an interior bedroom. There are no windows, no means of escape, but at least it's roomy, comfortable, and contains a bed.

There's no sign of a bathroom, which means either they're expecting us to use a piss pot, or more likely, they'll let us out, one at a time, to use the bathroom. Which is probably our one chance at escape.

Harper is the one who should try to get away.

Not only because she's *my wife,* but because she's *pregnant.*

She's resting her head on the pillow, lying above the blankets on the plush mattress after being practically electrocuted by the device around her neck.

I'll need to find a way to disarm it.

"Luca." Her voice is soft, and she mumbles as she pats the bed beside her. She's only been resting for a few short minutes.

I'm still surveying every inch of our new prison, trying to determine what I might use as a weapon, an escape tool, or even a way to disarm the necklace Harper wears.

If she's going to escape, we need to get that off of her or, at the very least, make it nothing more than a glorified fashion piece.

"Rest," I say and glance up at the camera. There is only one in the room, nestled in the corner. I slip out of my shoe and remove my sock, tossing it over the lens, bathing the camera in darkness.

That should work for a while, until one of the guards removes it.

When Harper is feeling better, I'll have her help me destroy it, but for now, it buys us a little time and privacy.

I scout every inch of the room, including the closet. There's no paneling, nothing to pry through, or an opening to sneak from one room to the next. I was hoping there might be access to an attic and then a window we might escape from.

Wishful thinking.

While the bulletproof vest and weapons have been taken from me, I'm still wearing the dark ensemble gifted to me by the guard downstairs.

I tap the camera that I'm still wearing, hoping it didn't get damaged. "Guys, anytime you want to rescue us, I'd be happy to get out of here. We both are ready to go home."

Harper slowly pushes herself to sit up.

"Who are you talking to?" she asks.

"Just myself," I say and glance at the covered surveillance camera. If there's audio attached, I don't want anyone discovering the hidden camera on me.

The guards only patted me down for weapons, my phone, that sort of thing before locking us inside on the second floor. They were careless, or maybe they believe I was stupid enough to come alone.

I did, after all, get caught.

"Right," Harper says and fully sits up on the mattress, pushing her legs to the edge of the bed. She glances at the mattress, a slight look of disgust filling her features.

Harper doesn't have to say a word about what happened because I know, I witnessed it.

Approaching the bed, I bring my hand to her cheek, grazing the skin, forcing her to look at me. "How long have you known?" I ask.

Her brow pinches.

My voice is soft, careful, not wanting to startle her. I caress her cheek, my legs gently nudging hers as I stand in front of her. "About the baby," I say, clarifying my question, because she's staring at me, awestruck.

Her face drains of all color, and she exhales a heavy breath. “How did you—never mind.” She grimaces and holds up a hand. There are tears in her eyes, unshed, and she rapidly blinks them away. “Now is not the time for that discussion.”

She’s right, if Livia can hear us, the last thing in the world I want is to give her any information that could be used to hurt Harper or anyone else I care about.

“Why do you think she brought us up here?” I ask.

The whole situation leaves me feeling more than just a little unsettled. She could have paraded us through the compound, back behind the locked metal gates. My gut tells me something’s amiss.

“To torture me all over again, or maybe torment you? She made it clear she wants my baby,” Harper whispers, casting her gaze down to her abdomen, and she rests a protective hand over her stomach. “She thinks it’s owed to her because of what happened to her husband.”

“She’s fucking wrong.” My jaw tightens, and I have to forcibly open my lips and breathe through my mouth to keep from grinding my teeth and cracking a tooth. “I won’t let them hurt you or our baby.”

“They—” Her voice goes quiet, barely above a whisper. She shuts her eyes, her bottom lip tugging between her teeth.

“You’re safe now,” I whisper, pressing a chaste kiss to her forehead. “No one will touch you again.”

“You know—about the doctor?” Harper asks, slowly, carefully, glancing up at me.

Sighing, I nod.

Her brow is tight, filled with confusion, and then she glances up at the covered camera in the room. “How?”

“We’ll talk about it later,” I assure her. I press one more kiss to her forehead and squeeze her hand before stepping away. The room is cold and empty without her in my reach.

I need to find us a way out of this room before one of the guards or Livia returns. I survey the room, checking every possible detail, latch, anything that might be useful to us.

"What are you looking for?" Harper asks, and I nod toward the cameras. While I've blinded the video, I don't know what can be heard. "Margaret told me that it's video surveillance only."

"Just in case, we should be cautious of what's being said."

Harper shrugs and forces herself to her feet. She expels a sigh and tilts her head, staring up at me. "Can you lift me up? I can try to disable it."

Making sure she's steady, I help Harper up onto my shoulders, and she removes the sock, dropping it onto my head while she yanks the wires forcibly out of the camera.

"It's disconnected," she says, her tone matter of fact.

"Can you rip it off the wall?" I ask. I don't want one of the guards trying to reassemble the device.

She wraps her fist around the camera, uses two hands and pulls with a steady force that sends me reeling as I grip my arms around her hips.

The camera pops off the wall, along with a good bit of plaster.

"Like this?" she asks, showing me the device, letting it dangle from her fingertips before dropping it to the floor with a loud smash.

I breathe with a sense of relief, knowing we're at least alone, minus the camera that I'm wearing.

I opt to keep it a secret, just in case there are any other hidden cameras in this place.

"Nice job," I tell her, helping Harper back down to the floor.

"Thanks. So, what's your plan, Einstein?" She glances me over, "because you getting caught and the two of us locked up in here doesn't seem like it was well thought out." Harper folds her arms across her chest.

The sassiness in her attitude is back, and I feel a sense of relief.

We'll get through this together.

"That obvious?" I ask, nose crinkling as I lean in and kiss her. "All I could think about was getting to you."

"Next time, rescue me. Don't join me in being held hostage. Okay?"

I'm glad she's still got her sense of humor. I steal another kiss; my fingers graze her cheek before they inadvertently touch the contraption around her neck.

"We need to work to get this off of you, or disarm it."

She laughs under her breath. "That would be great. It doesn't exactly go with my wardrobe."

There's sarcasm in her tone, and I brush a stray hair behind her ear, finding myself unable to stop touching her.

She's alive.

She's here with me.

While neither of us is out of harm's way—yet—for now, she's safe.

And I intend to keep her that way, protected.

Letting go of her feels wrong, but I back away, heading for the closet, searching the empty space, not finding anything I can use. There is a dresser and desk, both of which are also empty; the drawers contain not even a hint of dust.

"What are you looking for?" Harper asks.

"A screwdriver, knife, something I might be able to use to pry that contraption off without hurting you."

I make sure that the camera hidden on my shirt gets a good view of the device. I want Rhys and the others to see it, to know that it needs to come off when we escape.

I'm not foolish enough to think there won't be a bloodbath in this place, but I won't let anything happen to Harper.

"I don't remember them putting it on me, I was unconscious—drugged," she whispers and grimaces. "It's been a hell of a day—two days, is it?"

I stride across the room, my hand instantly on her cheek, caressing her as she stares up at me with a worried gaze.

"I won't let anything happen to you," I say.

It's a promise.

A vow.

She nods into my touch, her eyelids flutter closed for a fraction of a second, and her warm arms envelop my body, crushing me.

"Please tell me you didn't come alone," she whispers against my ear.

I want to tell her that our friends are just outside, planning and helping aid in our escape. But I can't help but worry the room is bugged and we have no privacy.

Even without the cameras, I can't know without a doubt that no one can eavesdrop on our conversation. And while I want to reassure her that Rhys, Ashton, and the others are devising a plan, I can't say the words aloud.

There's no pen or paper within the confines of the room.

No way for me to pass notes to her.

I smile wordlessly, hoping she understands. I press a finger to my lips to warn her that I don't trust that we're alone.

Technically, Rhys and the others are watching us, but that isn't what gives me reason to pause. It's that Livia and her men likely have hidden surveillance equipment tucked into the room. If there was one camera, there's likely to be more.

"Well, that sucks," she mutters, her eyes twinkling with mirth.

Harper understands to play along.

Good girl.

The bedroom door swings open without warning, and Livia stands with two guards at her side at the entrance to the bedroom door. "Bring the girl to me," she commands.

I shove Harper behind me, doing everything possible to protect her.

"Take me instead." I step forward, blocking the door and Harper from being dragged out of the room.

Livia laughs, the sound making my stomach plummet as she tilts her head, sizing me up. "Sweet offer, but you can't give us what we need."

The guard on the left steps forward, shoving me aside and stands, blocking my way as the other guard grabs Harper's arm, forcing her to come with him.

"Leave my wife alone!" I shout at the guard, grabbing the weapon he's holding slung across his chest and reaching for the gun trigger.

I'm too slow.

Harper's scream echoes through the room as Livia holds the small black remote in her hands, pushing the button, watching mercilessly as my wife collapses to the floor.

The necklace makes a crackling sound as Harper's screams rip through my heart. The guard bends down, putting Harper over his shoulder as he carries her out of the room.

"No!" I shout, lunging for the guard carrying my wife, when the other guard blocking me coldcocks me with his gun, knocking me backward, the pain rippling across my face, throbbing.

The guard slams the door in my face with a laugh.

I curse, my fists banging furiously on the door to be let out. "Take me with you!" I scream into the void.

TWENTY-ONE

NOVA

I stare at the screen in horror as Harper is thrown over the shoulder of one of the guards and disappears through the door.

Luca is safe, for now.

He's locked in a bedroom, by the looks of it, and he'll probably have a nice shiner on his cheek, but he appears to be relatively unharmed.

Harper is the one I'm worried about. We have no idea where they're taking her. And to find out she's pregnant, holy shit!

Liam stares at the tablet in front of him, watching video of Luca, a direct line of video and audio from the small hidden camera Luca has been wearing.

How long must we wait before doing something? I'm beginning to feel a bit on edge, like Luca, wanting to go in and rescue my family.

From the distance, we can see the property, but we're far enough away not to be noticed.

I have an unsettling feeling as the third vehicle I've seen in the past twenty minutes has pulled up at the property. They're all different models of vehicles, clearly pricey, fancy.

Ashton seems engrossed in his phone. "What's so important that you're staring at your cell phone instead of helping?"

I can't help but feel annoyed. My brother and best friend's lives are in danger, and Ashton is playing on his stupid cell phone.

Ashton's jaw clenches and his gaze flickers from his phone briefly to me. He lifts the device, showing me a live breaking news feed. "Harper's parents went to the local news about her abduction. It's making national news."

Rhys curses under his breath and grabs the phone from Ashton's hands, turning the volume up to hear what's being said.

"This doesn't change anything." I glance between the boys. "We need to go in and rescue Harper and Luca. We know they're both inside, and if there's any chance they plan on moving them or—"

Ashton shoots a glance in my direction. "I thought you wanted nothing to do with us—this." He gestures at the equipment in front of him. "And now you're giving orders?"

"Someone has to do something!"

Right now, we need all the help that we can get, especially after my dumbass brother decided to waltz right in through the front door.

What the hell was he thinking?

Oh, right, he wasn't thinking. He found out his wife is pregnant.

Liam's attention is transfixed on the tablet, making sure if we're given any hint of a clue, we don't miss it.

I saunter up to Liam, standing beside him, getting a glimpse of Luca.

He's still alive.

My heart pounds as I watch him.

I'm grateful, the camera seems to have gone unnoticed by Livia's crew. Luca paces back and forth after pounding on the door for the past several minutes. He's locked up tight in that room, which at least isn't a prison cell.

"I'm more concerned about the newcomers," Liam says and glances up, pointing at the compound as two more vehicles head for the driveway.

He hands the tablet to Sophia.

"More patrols?" Sophia asks and returns her attention to the tablet, in case there's anything of interest to report to us.

Rhys is busy cataloging the cameras and interior surveillance footage. He's making it easy for him to swap feeds, while still having access to cameras that we may not need at the moment but that could become important later on for us.

Rhys zooms in on the exterior cameras housed right outside the main entrance of the compound. "I don't know who these people are, but they're not security. They're dressed up like they're attending a gala."

"Given what we know about their previous business ventures, I'd presume it's an auction," Ashton says. "We know they're in the business of abducting women and children. We've already seen several girls being held inside the compound."

My mouth runs dry. "Human trafficking," I rasp, feeling albeit a bit woozy. I don't like that my best friend and brother are both locked up inside that place. I glance at the screen Sophia is holding. While I can't see Luca's face, he's moving around, inspecting every inch of that room.

At least he's alive.

My phone buzzes with a text alert, and I yank it from my back pocket, surprised to learn that my father is awake.

Relief floods through me. But it's nowhere near over.

He still has a long road ahead of him for recovery, and then there are Harper and Luca, who aren't out of danger yet.

Rhys clears his throat. "I think it's safe to assume they're here to buy the girls we saw who were locked in with Harper when Luca first arrived."

I shove my phone away. "What are we going to do to stop them?" I ask.

Rescuing Harper and Luca may be our priority, but we can't just walk away from knowing that countless girls are locked up inside, being held against their will.

"We can't do anything until we know how to disable those collars," Rhys says, his attention entirely on the screen in front of him.

"What about an EMP? If we were able to deliver a small pulse that would interfere with electronics, it should take out the collars on all the girls," Ashton says.

"Do you know how to make one?" I raise an eyebrow, giving him my undivided attention. The idea is solid, but it's not like we have an EMP how-to-guide with the weapons we've procured.

"I don't think any of us know how or have the necessary tools," Rhys says. "But Dante's guy may have something we can rig up with the materials he's provided us. I'm waiting for a call back."

I huff under my breath. "Sure, because we have all the time in the world. It's just Luca and Harper's lives we're talking about." My moodiness knows no bounds, and Ashton reaches out, his hand caressing the small of my back, a soft yet intimate gesture, and I can feel his stare.

I should pull away from him, but I don't.

I want to stay angry, but the truth of it is, he's here now, willing to risk his life to save Luca and Harper. I can't say the same about the other guys I've dated in the past.

Several more cars pull up, and I glance over Rhys's shoulder at the footage from inside the house. "They're moving Harper and the other girls," I say. The camera feed has them moving farther inside the house. I grab the map that we've outlined from what we've seen and grab a pencil, continuing to fill it in with the location of where they're taking Harper and the others.

They escort the girls to a small room, forcing them to change attire. It appears Livia is there, shouting out orders, but we don't have audio from the surveillance feeds, only video.

The audio feed that we do have is tied to Luca's microphone and he's an entire floor away from Harper.

I study every movement, try to keep track of how many girls there are being held captive. In addition to Harper and the girls, there are also several older ladies who are stationed in small sections, doing hair and makeup.

It's definitely an auction of some kind.

There's no reason they'd be dolling up the girls for sport. In a matter of minutes, the girls are shucked from one room to the next.

"They're on the move again," I say, relaying the most up-to-date information to the team.

The girls are shuffled down the hallway, remaining on the first floor, and make a hard left as they head in the opposite direction of where we're located. The guard opens the double wooden doors, shoving those inside who don't move quickly enough. They're locked in a room near the back of the compound.

The room has ceiling-to-floor windows, but the view leads to a garden located within the courtyard of the compound. Sunlight shines in through the windows, basking the room in a bright glow.

The wall opposite has no evidence of windows or the outside, but based on my sketch and the video footage we've gained access to, I'm fairly confident it's an exterior wall. Almost like they intended for this room to appear deep inside the compound.

There are semi-circular, dark-red velvet booths and cherry wooden tables throughout the room. At the far end, against the exterior wall, is a bar. Chandelier lighting hangs overhead but is currently dimly lit, with most of the light coming from the windows to the garden.

The girls huddle together, frightened, like they know what's about to come next.

Rhys grabs his phone that is ringing; it's Jaxson Monroe from the caller I.D. screen. I glance at Ashton, staring up at him. "We can't just sit out here and wait. We have to do something," I whisper, pleading with him.

Watching is torture. Anxiety is mounting and I just want to rush through the open door and shoot all the bastards who are holding my friends against their will.

That must have been how Luca felt, knowing Harper was locked up inside.

Powerless.

“We need to take control,” I say, glancing from the compound to Ashton. “Please, tell me you have a plan.”

He wanted this life, working in the mafia, following in his father’s footsteps. Now is his time to shine and prove that this is what he intends to do and why it matters.

Because if anything happens to either one of them locked up inside—

My breath catches in my throat, and I force away the slight tremor in my hands. “Ashton.” Urgency laces my voice.

“I’m thinking,” Ashton says, and glances at Rhys, who hurries to the trunk of the vehicle with all sorts of equipment we’ve been provided.

Rhys puts in a Bluetooth earpiece so he can hear Jaxson while he tinkers with three different devices, one of which is an explosive.

Hesitantly, I take a step back.

I don't know what the hell Rhys is planning, but I don't want to keep getting hurt. Already, I'm aching inside, my heart bleeding at the fact everyone I care about is in danger.

"Ashton, give me a hand," Rhys orders and has him help make some modifications while I stalk over toward Sophia.

I glance at the tablet in her hands. Luca keeps yanking on the door handle in the room where he's being held, but it's locked. Without any windows, there isn't another way out of that room.

"How large a blast radius are we looking at?" Rhys asks.

I glance back over my shoulder at him, already knowing what's going to happen, and I can't say I'm happy about it. But whatever it takes to save Harper and Luca.

Sophia places a hand on my shoulder. "We'll get them back."

I roll my lips together and wordlessly nod. Right, we'll get them back. But then what? With the DeLucas, it seems a never-ending battle. We need to stop them once and for all.

I heard Harper's words to Luca; Livia wants their child.

When will it end?

"How do we detonate it?" Rhys asks over the earpiece, and his eyes tighten for a fraction of a second. "Okay. We'll be in touch." He removes the earpiece and shoves his phone into his pocket.

"What's the plan?" Ashton asks, glancing at Rhys.

"We need to make sure that we use the explosive device before the EMP, or one of us will manually have to detonate it." Rhys doesn't so much as glance at me.

"Sophia, can you man the drone if we load the explosives and the EMP to it?"

She hands me the tablet, letting me keep an eye on

Luca. "I don't think we'll be able to detonate more than one at a time," Sophia says.

"That's okay, we can have you put the explosive in position and wait to detonate until the EMP is in place." Rhys clicks his tongue. "But I'll need you and Nova to stay here while we infiltrate the compound and make sure that we get Harper and Luca out."

"You're leaving us here because we're girls, aren't you?" I glare at Rhys.

"I'm leaving you here to watch the video feed and report to us what you see, at least until the EMP detonates. If they move Harper or Luca, we need to know about it."

"And once the cameras are disabled?" I ask. "What then? The moment the EMP hits, the cameras are worthless. And you want us to detonate the EMP immediately after, right?"

Rhys loads up the explosive, securing it to the drone while Sophia flies it over the property, careful not to be seen. He has her carefully place the device near the backside of the compound, closer to the girl's location and the garden, intending to blast a hole through the wall to let them escape.

No one notices the drone, too busy planning their little party, while Sophia brings the drone back and Rhys secures the EMP to it.

"Wait!" Ashton interjects, "we're going to have to detonate before we bring the EMP over, or else we're risking it getting damaged in the explosion. We only have one chance to pull this off."

"He's right," I say. "We don't know how big a blast radius the explosion will be."

I hope that it's far enough away to leave an exit for the girls without hurting them.

"Right. Good thinking," Rhys says and pats Ashton's shoulder. "I'll load up the EMP. Wait to send it over until after the explosion. Detonate it as soon as you get it in position."

The EMP is in position in the drone, and Sophia hides behind the vehicle with me as we watch the camera footage. Luca hasn't left his room. The girls are still locked up in the ballroom.

Rhys hands me the trigger for the EMP. "Wait until it's in position, then activate it as soon as you can."

"Okay," I say, my fingers cold and trembling as I take the black trigger with a red button. The weight feels overwhelming.

Rhys, Ashton, and Liam gather supplies and gear, pulling on bulletproof vests and weapons, packing up with extra bullets, knives, and daggers. Any extra space is utilized with gear. They hunker down behind the SUV.

Rhys counts down from three and uses the detonator, blowing a massive hole in the building. The ground quakes at our feet, smoke bellows and rises.

I press a chaste kiss to Ashton's lips. "Be careful," I warn while Sophia uses the remote control, bringing the drone up into the air and toward the compound.

Rhys, Liam, and Ashton hurry across the open expanse toward the compound. Clad in black and decked out with weapons, they definitely stand out.

As soon as Sophia can get the drone into position, we have orders to detonate the EMP.

Girls are running, fleeing from the hole we blasted through the building's wall. Sophia lowers the EMP near the explosion, and I hit the trigger.

I expect static to fill the screens.

Instead, everything is dead.

The computer with every camera we had access to, dark.

The tablet, not so much as a hint of battery.

It's as though everything is off. I retrieve my phone from my pocket.

Dead.

Sophia glances at my phone. "Was that supposed to happen?" she asks. "How far did the EMP reach?"

TWENTY-TWO

HARPER

The explosion rocks the building, debris and smoke wafting in every direction.

Most of the girls look around, frantic, the wall crumbling, gleaming with sunlight, revealing a glimpse of outside.

Freedom is just a few feet away.

The chandelier swings haphazardly, and I glance up, hurrying away from the center of the room as it falls to the ground, smashing into a thousand tiny pieces, the crystal shards spraying in every direction.

I make sure to keep my back to the chandelier as it pelts the ground, the crystal showering us like bullets, and one of them grazes my arm and another my cheek. It tears the yellow chiffon dress that Livia made me wear. She made all the girls dress in bright colors for the "festivities" of the evening.

Yellows, reds, and oranges.

None of which were random.

She had several older ladies fix our hair and apply makeup. They wouldn't speak to us, would barely make eye contact. And every time I attempted to glean information, they'd shock me with that stupid little remote trigger.

Livia made sure that we each wore a specific gown and were told not to trade dresses.

Her tone adamant as she threw clothes at each of us. If I had to guess, the colors were grouped by age. Margaret and I both wear yellow. The younger girls are wearing orange, and two girls who are definitely younger than us but the same age as the girls in orange, wore red.

Margaret whispered to me that those girls were new,

but she wasn't sure why I was in yellow and they were in red.

It didn't matter. I was getting the hell out of this nightmare and not waiting around for whatever would happen next.

Light gleams into the ballroom.

Luca didn't come alone.

Billowing smoke quickly fills the space, and I cough, a younger girl wearing orange is just on the other side of the glass, a sea of pain between us. Her eyes search around the room frantically for another way of escape.

The windows leading to the courtyard shattered with the explosion. There's glass everywhere and none of us are wearing shoes. Each girl is careful as they hurry through the wall, broken stucco offering a glimpse outside. There isn't much room to squeeze through, but it's enough to let one girl escape at a time.

Crystal and glass crunch beneath my feet, and I ignore the pain as it slices at my skin. I won't leave anyone behind. I hurry over to help the younger girl in orange having her wrap her arms around my neck and her legs around my hips as I take the brunt of the pain, walking over what feels like hot coals as the bottoms of my feet get sliced up.

I make it just over the glass, putting the young girl in orange's feet firmly on the ground. "Go!" I urge, not wanting anyone to waste a valuable second.

"Stop!" Livia's voice beckons from inside the compound, and the force of electricity burns through my neck, bringing me to my knees.

I'm not the only one she's torturing.

The girls inside collapse around me, the pain unbearable. It hurts to breathe, to merely exist.

Heavy footfalls of boots storm the grounds; they're just outside the hallway behind the mafia boss.

The fire alarm blares at an annoying rate until it suddenly goes eerily silent.

The smoke hasn't vanished.

There aren't sprinklers to put out the fire.

A soft click and the collar around my neck unlatches, loosening just slightly at the same moment that the fire alarm ceases to function. I bring my hands to my neck, removing the device, throwing it across the room, letting it hit the wall, hoping to break it so no one will ever be forced to wear such a monstrosity again.

We don't have much time. I hurry to the torn apart stucco wall, helping the girls out as quickly as possible.

Two more girls slip through to the outside as the men brandishing guns storm into the chaos.

I cough in the smoke, the air thick and heavy, enough to make it difficult to see, but I can hear Livia shouting out orders to her crew. "Don't shoot her! She's pregnant with *my baby.*"

If she doesn't want us dead, then this is our one chance at escape. Practically pushing the girls outside, I wait until they've all gotten out before I begin to wedge myself through the crack, the bright light nearly blinding as I glance back at Livia just a few feet away, rushing toward me.

Luca.

He's still inside.

The inward struggle makes me stall for a split second.

“Come on,” one of the girls shouts, grabbing my arm, yanking me through the hole and outside. “We have to move!”

TWENTY-THREE

ASHTON

Coms are down. There's smoke billowing from the opposite side of the compound. We have to trust that Harper will be able to find her way out. Without video or audio surveillance, we're going in blind. The EMP makes sure of that the moment we approach the house.

Rhys directs the team, taking lead as we sneak in through the main door. It's unlocked, left open perhaps for the guests in attendance.

There haven't been any new arrivals in the past few minutes, though I imagine if anyone had been planning on coming and saw the smoke, they likely turned away.

I've memorized the map, our blueprint for rescuing Luca. It seems Rhys has, as well, as he leads up the staircase and we hug the wall, careful not to be seen.

There are no smoke detectors going off due to the EMP, and it's a welcome relief not hearing the blasted high-pitch scream as we hurry down the hallway.

There are men storming downstairs, running and shouting out orders, but none of them notice us. They're too busy dealing with the girls escaping, which concerns me regarding Harper, but there are only three of us and splitting up is a piss-poor idea.

I glance up at the camera in the hallway, grateful that's permanently disabled.

Every door is shut in the hallway, and we make it to the room we believe Luca is being held captive. Rhys glances back at me, making sure I'm in agreement.

I offer a brief nod, confident that we've approached the right door.

Rhys retrieves a lockpick from his pocket. He works quickly at it before turning the handle, slowly opening the door.

I hurry closer as he opens the door, poking my head in to make sure it is, in fact, the correct room. "Luca," I quietly shout, trying to keep my voice down but grab his attention.

His eyes widen and he hurries like a bolt of lightning right out of the room. "Did you hear that explosion?" Luca asks, glancing past me as he comes out into the hallway. "Where's Harper?"

"Hopefully, she made it out," I say, biting my tongue. There were a lot of guards, and it sounded as though all of them were heading toward the girls.

"You didn't rescue her first?" Luca's eyes widen, and I hand him a pistol from my hip, giving him a weapon to defend himself.

"We don't have time for idle chit-chat," Rhys says as he turns and heads back down the stairs toward the front door. It's still unguarded, which is lucky for us.

"Where are you guys going?" Luca hisses, chasing after Rhys. He grabs him by the arm, shoving him around. "Harper is that way!" He points in the opposite direction where Harper had been kept locked behind the iron gate.

"If we're lucky, she made it out. We blew a hole in the wall. We have to trust that she can handle her own. We'll catch up with her outside, where we have better odds." Rhys gestures for the door and we sneak out.

Gunfire erupts, and I wince. Knowing Harper is still out there makes my stomach flop. I chance a quick glance at Luca and he's steaming.

Rhys steps out first, making sure no one is waiting to ambush us and then we skirt around the property in the opposite direction that we came before sneaking around the compound. We make our way in the direction of the smoke, the plumes cast high overhead, not the least bit slowing down.

Smoke fills the air, the wind whipping it in our direction, making the air hazy and thick. I choke on the smoke, eyes watering, and my throat burning, but I ignore the discomfort.

We need to find Harper.

Luca stumbles in front of me over a rock, and I reach out to grab his arm.

"I'm fine," he grumbles, managing to catch himself before he face plants.

Immediately, I let go and offer a nod. Luca keeps the gun between both hands, pointed downward as we skirt the edge of the compound. The exterior is a beige stucco, and as we gather closer to the area of the explosion, there are flames licking the exterior of the building, climbing like ivy over the walls.

Girls flee in several directions, but there's no sign of Harper.

Gunshots erupt from inside the building, and that's when I catch sight of her golden hair and soot-coated skin. There's ash falling across the blonde tresses and flecks of blood speckled to her like freckles.

"Harper!" Luca shouts, gathering her attention as she slides through the exterior wall with the help of another girl.

Rhys is there first, his gun poised while Luca offers Harper a hand, the other girl in a bright orange dress with darker hair and sullen eyes skirts back, hands up, and hurries away from us, perhaps worried that we're the enemy.

I don't chase after her.

I'm right at Luca's side as he lifts Harper into his arms, carrying her back to our vehicle. She's covered in abrasions, blood caked to her hair, her shoulder, and her yellow dress is torn.

"Put me down!" I hear her insistence, and Luca carefully places her feet on the ground, an arm around her as they hurry away.

She's limping, clearly injured, but between the two of them, they're able to run faster with her in pain than Luca carrying her.

Rhys and I cover the blasted exit. Livia and guards pour rounds of bullets, poking further holes in the stucco, destroying what's left of the wall outside as we stand our ground.

Luca and Harper are already around the corner when I feel the impact, the sudden blow of a bullet to my chest.

I'm knocked to the ground, the wind stolen from my lungs as Rhys bends down, grabbing my vest to look at the bullet and see if it pierced my skin.

The pain, the bruise, it aches, but that's all I'm feeling. I need to take off the vest to be certain, but not now, not while we're under gunfire.

"We need to move. Can you get up?" Rhys asks.

Grimacing, I'm up and he's covering us with rounds of bullets as we dart back against the stucco wall, around the property, fleeing in haste.

The sound of gunshots lull to a nothingness.

But I worry it's far from over. "We need to stop them," I say, glancing at Rhys.

"Can you make it back to the car?"

He's crazy if he thinks he can go up against all of them. There are too many men of DeLuca's men still alive. "I'm not leaving you," I say.

"That's an order, not a request. Get back to the others. Make sure the car still runs. If not, you'd better come up with an exit plan, fast." Sweat drips from his forehead and I hurry across the front of the property before running as swiftly as possible, my legs burning; my chest still aches, but I'm alive.

Gasping for breath as I reach Luca and the others, I hang my head, trying to catch my breath.

"Where's Rhys?" Nova asks.

A second explosion erupts, tearing the compound apart, the building crumbles and dust rising up into the sky.

"Shit." I stare at the explosion, the dust, the smoke and fire rising up as ashes catch in the wind.

Anyone remaining inside the compound is likely trapped and buried under the rubble or dead.

Smoke fills the area, the wind kicking it in our direction, making it impossible to see the compound or what's left of it.

"We need to get the car started," I say, jumping into the front seat and trying the engine.

It's dead.

"The EMP took it out," Nova says. "Also burned out my cell phone. We're stuck here."

TWENTY-FOUR

BRISTOL

Jaxson curses as he runs a hand through his dark, cropped hair. His cheeks are red, eyes fuming, and he glances at me. Like somehow, I'm to blame.

He's got the news on, and the breaking story changes from Harper's abduction to an EMP in Nevada that has darkened a great deal of Las Vegas.

The city and Las Vegas Strip remain untouched, but the outskirts of Las Vegas are dark.

"We need to get them out, ASAP. I can't let this come back on us." Jaxson stands from his desk, his chair squeaking against the floor as he hurries out of his office.

I chase after him. "Where are you going?"

Until Liam returns home, he's in danger.

He hasn't reached out, and with the EMP, he likely won't, unless his phone was enclosed in a faraday cage.

So far, there's been no communication from any of them since the blast.

I wring my hands together, anxiety creeping up on me, and I sway, my hand clasping the doorjamb, hoping to go unnoticed. Nausea packs one hell of a punch, and I exhale, doing everything in my power to slow my racing heart.

But it's not like I have any control over it.

The medicine works, on most days, but this type of fear, the crippling variety, doesn't exactly help matters.

Stress makes everything worse.

Jaxson stalks into Mason's office, slamming the door shut behind himself.

It's clear I'm not invited to their little debrief of current events. I gnaw at my bottom lip, waiting seconds feels like minutes. I hurry back into Jaxson's office, hoping there will be an update on the news, something worthwhile.

Through the glass window of his office, the shades are drawn, and I catch sight of Jaxson storming back toward me.

"Any news?"

"Mason is getting a chopper out to them."

Slowly, I nod, falling back into the chair I sat in earlier. Rubbing my hands on my pants, I'm sweating profusely and fan myself. The room is stifling, but I know without a doubt it's me. My internal thermostat is broken.

Fear grips my heart, clutching it, squeezing, and I gasp for breath.

Jaxson glances at me and then turns up the volume on the television as we watch the news report. "I want you to scour the message boards, social media, let me know what people saw—what they're saying."

It's a distraction, not a great one, but it will keep me busy. I retrieve my phone and start scrolling.

Immediately, the news threads are filled with conspiracies and wild theories.

There aren't any physical accounts of events.

At least not yet. Anyone in the EMP blast zone, their electronics were fried.

"Most of the discussion is that people think the government is behind the EMP."

"Wouldn't be the worst place to put the blame. It is their technology," Jaxson mutters. "There's an air force base not far from where the EMP went off. We might be able to push that narrative."

"You want us to lie?" I stare at him, surprised. I've always thought of Jaxson as the golden retriever type. Loyal. Honest. A golden boy.

"It's better than the government coming here asking questions, or worse, showing up on the Ricci's doorstep, asking how they got their hands on the EMP technology. Because Dante wouldn't so much as blink before turning us over to save himself."

"How noble of him," I mutter.

"I never said he was noble."

Jaxson's phone rings, and he answers it, momentarily ignoring me. "Yes, we need an extraction." He pauses. "At least seven."

I purse my lips, eyes widening, listening in to Jaxson's conversation as I stare at my phone.

"I'll send you the coordinates now. But you need to get there before anyone notices there's an explosion and they send in the cavalry."

TWENTY-FIVE

HARPER

My feet are sliced, and they burn as though they're on fire. I keep a firm grip on Luca, my arms around him as though he's a physical part of my body, afraid that if I let go, I may still be inside, locked up.

Luca is safe.

Alive.

He kisses my lips, pulls me tighter as we're huddled behind the dead vehicle.

"The EMP fried everything," Ashton grumbles as he tosses his dead cell phone into the trunk of the SUV.

"If Livia has another team or anyone who survived, we're an enormous target out here."

"We've been here the entire time, and there's been no sign of anyone leaving that building," Sophia says.

"The girls got out on the opposite side," I say. "They're fleeing on foot. If any guards survived, they'll probably hunt them down."

"Even if Livia is dead?" Liam asks.

Ashton keeps his gun ready, poised if any guards come rushing at us through the thick blanket of smoke. "It's doubtful anyone survived that second explosion."

"Including Rhys," Nova whispers, and her breath falters. Her eyes flicker with pain, like she's holding back tears.

The sound of rotor blades from a helicopter are heard overhead as I squint and glance up into the sky.

"That's a fucking Black Hawk," Ashton mutters.

The helicopter lands a short distance away. There's

no helipad, just dirt. Luca curses under his breath, his brow furrowed with worry.

Ashton glances at me, like I'm somehow to blame for this mess.

One of the pilots disembarks and hurries in our direction. "I hear you need a ride."

We glance at one another, unsure who sent the helicopter, but being stranded is far worse. "Come on," Ashton says, gesturing for all of us to follow the pilot as we hurry toward the helicopter.

I keep hold of Luca's hand as we head into the helicopter, glancing around, wondering if we're about to be detained for questioning by the government.

"Is this everyone?" the pilot asks as he counts six aloud. "I was told there would be seven."

"Rhys never came out," Ashton says, and I wince, the weight of my abduction feels incredibly heavy, as though I'm in part to blame. Had he not come here to rescue me, he'd still be alive.

I glance at Nova as she climbs into the seat across from me, and the guilt consumes me. Her eyes are red, glassy. Ashton steals the seat next to her, buckling in. His hand finds her thigh, giving it a reassuring squeeze.

The moment feels entirely too intimate for me to be watching them, and I glance away. I shift in my seat, my seatbelt tight as I glance at Luca seated beside me. "Thank you."

"For?"

"Coming to get me," I say.

He laughs and shakes his head. "Do you think there was another option?"

We land back at the airfield and take the private plane back home.

It feels empty, wrong to not have Rhys onboard. The mood is heavy, stoic, and the air is thick, making my heart ache for Nova.

While I didn't personally know Rhys, it's impossible to ignore her soft tears and pain-laced tone as she leans into Ashton's embrace.

He hugs her, pulling her into his lap as we reach cruising altitude on our way home.

I may not be to blame for the abduction, but I still feel the weight of guilt, like it's my fault, because if they hadn't come rescue me, he'd have never died.

"You're quiet," Luca says, his hand running soothingly up and down my arm, his gaze intent on me, but I'm lost in my own thoughts and Nova's pain keeps washing over me like a tidal wave.

"Just looking forward to going home, seeing Zeke," I whisper and force a smile.

"Are we going to talk about what happened in there?" Luca asks, his gaze intent on me, but I can't meet his stare. I don't want him to feel pity for what occurred. I'd rather not think about that doctor or the intrusive exam.

Grimacing, I pull my arm away from his touch, folding my arms across my chest.

Luca glances down, his brow tightening as he unbuckles his seatbelt and notices the crimson on the floor of the plane. "You're bleeding."

"It's nothing."

He slowly lifts my ankle, taking a long look at the bottoms of my feet. Luca curses and shakes his head. "You should have told me. I wouldn't have let you walk at all if I'd known you were injured."

Luca heads toward the back of the plane, and a few minutes later, he returns with a first-aid kit. He unzips the container, retrieving a handful of items, sorting through them until he's satisfied with what he's found.

"Everything okay?" Liam asks, unbuckling his seatbelt and coming to stand with Luca. He squats down to look at the bottoms of my feet and grimaces. "Ouch."

I snort at his response. "I don't think it's hurting you any," I say and force a smile. I appreciate both of their concern, but it's unwarranted. I'll be fine.

Unlike Rhys.

I cast my glance up at Nova. Her eyes are red, puffy, and she avoids my stare. Her gaze is trained on the ground. Ashton's strong arms embrace her, and he's whispering something into her ear, holding her against him.

It's obvious how much Ashton still cares for Nova, even though they're broken up.

Unless something changed between them. It's hard to tell from just glancing in their direction. They look so close, tight-knit, but Nova told me how she didn't want that life after college.

How she wanted someone who wouldn't become her father.

Luca rests my ankle on his knee while he's bent down in front of me, inspecting my foot, making sure there isn't any glass or crystal imbedded.

Liam hands him a set of tweezers, and my eyes widen. "What do you plan on doing with those?" I ask, already knowing the answer. But I want to be wrong.

My feet are sore, but they don't hurt terribly with my feet up while seated on the airplane.

"You have slivers of glass that need to be removed."

"Since when are you a doctor?" I scoff and yank my foot away from him.

Liam grabs the seat next to me where Luca was sitting. "We've sterilized the tweezers. We need to get the glass out and then disinfect the wound, so it doesn't get infected."

"And it can't wait until we get back?" I huff.

"It can, but are you going to let me carry you off the airplane?" Luca asks.

TWENTY-SIX

LUCA

Of course, Harper won't let me carry her off the airplane or inside the compound when we arrive back at my parents' house.

Her feet are thoroughly bandaged, and she tries to hide the limping, but the bottoms of her feet are ravaged.

I'd like her to see a doctor or get checked out at the hospital after what she's been through, but that's a fight I'm not ready to have with her and there would be a lot of questions.

"Luca!" my father's voice bellows through the hall and there's a breath of relief that I recognize when I see him. "Harper," he says and nods, pleased to see her as well.

Harper brushes past him, heading straight for the playroom. "Where's Zeke?"

"He's with Paige and Nikki."

"Did they go to the park?" I ask, glancing around. It's chilly outside, but there's still daylight.

My father sighs and shakes his head. "They were meeting with a lawyer on your behalf."

"A lawyer?" Harper glances from my father to me. "What about?"

"We should probably discuss what happened, but we'll need to speak with the police. Your parents, Harper, called the local sheriff's office and reported your disappearance. It's been all over the local news, and they've been insisting on taking full-custody of Zeke."

"What?" Her eyes widen and my stomach bottoms out.

"Don't worry," he says, nodding for us to follow to his office.

I keep an arm wrapped around her waist. She's slow as she walks, the pain inevitable, but she winces through it. My wife is definitely stubborn.

"Your parents previously had custody of your son," Dante says.

"Yes," Harper says with a faint nod. "He's in my custody now."

"Well, since you were missing, they decided to challenge Luca's custodial rights since he's not Zeke's biological son and were intending to take our family to court on Monday."

"Tomorrow," I whisper, glancing at Harper.

My father leads us to his office, opening the door and waiting for us to enter before closing it behind us. I let Harper take the closest chair, not wanting her to be on her feet any longer than absolutely necessary.

Her gaze tightens. "Well, I'm home now. My parents aren't getting custody of Zeke. If something were to happen to me..." Harper says and glances at me as she sits.

I interrupt her before she can finish her thought. "I would get custody of Zeke, wouldn't I? We're married." I take a seat beside her, reaching for her hand, giving it a squeeze.

My father sighs. "It's not that simple. Harper would need a will specifying who Zeke's legal guardian would be. Do you have one?"

Wordlessly, she shakes her head.

"In that case, Zeke's biological father or grandparents could gain custody. A stepparent would be a last resort, especially if a biological family member were petitioning for custody."

"That's fucked up," I grumble. "Zeke is *my* son."

"And that's why we were consulting an attorney, because your parents made it abundantly clear that we had to hand Zeke over to them. We refused. There were a few colorful words exchanged, and I fully anticipated being served custody papers Monday morning; it's why I had the girls seek out an experienced attorney."

Harper squeezes my hand, her gaze set on me. "Your father is right. We should draw up a living will."

"That's not good enough," I say. A living will only has any merit when Harper is dead. Not only do I *not* want to think about that, what about if she's incapacitated? "I want to legally adopt Zeke. He's my son too."

"We can have the lawyer draw up the papers," my father says, glancing at Harper, "as long as you're in agreement."

"Of course," Harper whispers and glances at me. "Are you sure?"

I can't believe she's asking me that, after all we've been through together. "One hundred percent. We're not separating our children."

"Children?" my father repeats and glances between us.

"Harper is pregnant," I say, breaking the news to Dante. A huge grin spreads across my face. It's not something we've discussed, but it happened, and we're married. There are far worse situations to be in, like where we were a couple of hours ago.

She pulls out of my touch. Her eyes narrow and her nostrils flare as she stands. "I really wish you hadn't just announced that to your father."

Not a doubt in my mind she's pissed. She doesn't so much as flinch from the abrasions on her feet as she glares at me, fuming and folds her arms across her chest. "I'm not sure I even want to keep it."

TWENTY-SEVEN

NOVA

The minute our flight lands and we're back at the compound, I jump in my car to head to the hospital to check on my father. I've heard that he's awake, out of the coma, but still being kept a few more days while he recovers.

"Wait up," Ashton says, chasing after me.

I raise an eyebrow as I unlock the passenger door.

He climbs in beside me, and I hit the gas long before he has time to buckle his seatbelt.

I'm in a hurry.

He clicks his seatbelt and adjusts his seat to get comfortable. “Slow down, speed demon,” Ashton jokes, but I’m not laughing.

It’s been a hellacious day. At least Harper is okay, but Rhys—just the mere thought of him running into that building and my eyes burn all over again.

“Your dad’s awake. He’s fine, slow down so we don’t end up in a bed beside him or a coffin,” he mutters.

“That’s not funny!” I glare at him, turning my attention briefly away from the road.

“Stop!” Ashton screams as I nearly plow through an intersection, missing the stop sign.

I slam on the brakes, my heart pounding haphazardly in my chest as I gasp for breath. “Shit,” I grumble, realizing my mistake. Thankfully, no one got hurt, but it could have been another disaster.

One is enough for today.

“How about I drive?” Ashton offers and I scoff at his suggestion.

“No thanks.”

I don't need him driving. I know how to get to the hospital, and I keep both hands on the steering wheel and avoid glancing at Ashton. He's too big of a distraction that I don't need. His silence is strangely comforting, and I concentrate on the road and traffic until we finally pull up at the hospital parking garage.

We head inside the hospital to the visitor's center, receiving a sticker badge that I affix to my shirt. Ashton does the same and then his hand falls to the small of my back as we follow the maze of hallways to the elevator.

His gesture sends a flutter through my body and I regrettably pull away, tapping the button for the elevator repeatedly.

"It won't come any faster when you do that." His voice is light, carefree, without a worry in the world.

Probably because I'm the one shouldering all of it.

I bite my tongue, and when the elevator dings, I exhale a breath and hurry inside, pressing the button for the eighth floor.

Ashton is right at my side, this time keeping his

hands to himself. He slides them into his pockets, glancing around awkwardly as we stand in silence.

The doors close and the ride up is anything but short or quiet.

Ashton hums and I raise an eyebrow, glancing in his direction.

I don't know what tune is going through his head or if he's making it up entirely. He keeps humming as I glare at him and he seems to ignore my irritability, like it doesn't exist.

The elevator dings as we reach the eighth floor and I step out first, glancing at the placard in the hallway to determine where I go from here to find my father's room.

It takes a second and then I make a right, another placard, another hallway. This time, I turn left and follow it until I get near the end of the hallway, across from the nurse's station. The door is closed and Halsey, dad's cousin, stands outside, playing bodyguard.

Halsey wordlessly nods for me to enter.

Even if he told me not to, there isn't much he could do to stop me. I'd throw my security dog, Ashton, at him.

I inwardly snicker at the mental image of Hasley and Ashton fighting and brush it aside as I open the hospital room door, stepping inside.

Dad is hooked up to monitors, machines, they're constantly buzzing and beeping, the sound and bright, stark halogen lights overwhelming.

Mom, surprisingly, isn't at his bedside. I didn't stick around long enough at the compound to see if she was home.

"Hey, you're awake," I say, stating the obvious. His head is bandaged with gauze wrapped around his forehead. The blood cleaned and gone from the shooting, but the evidence still staring right back at me.

Dad breathes a sigh of relief when he sees me and pushes the button on the bed to sit up farther. "Come in." He waves me into the room.

Ashton is on my heels, right behind me, holding the door when I let go and stalk around to the opposite side of the hospital bed, taking a seat in the nearby vacant chair.

"It's good to see you, sir. You're looking much better," Ashton says.

Dad almost gives a smile, more of a half-smirk, and glances from Ashton to me. "I hear you both went to Las Vegas. I swear if you got married—" There's a tone in his voice that shows both concern and is laced with something else.

Anger?

I'm unsure. It makes my stomach flop.

He doesn't know about the breakup.

"We didn't," Ashton says, quick to settle any confusion. "We went with the others to rescue Harper. Do you remember her abduction?"

Dad shakes his head no and winces. "I saw it on the television this morning. Is she—all right?"

"She's fine," I say, and my voice catches in my throat as I reach for Dad's hand. He's the only one who might understand what I'm feeling. "Rhys went with us..." my voice trails off.

The air heavy, my breath hitches.

"He didn't make it," Ashton says, saying the words that I can't seem to voice aloud.

Dad nods, his brow furrowed, and his nose crinkles slightly at his obvious discomfort. "That's unfortunate. Rhys was a good man. Always looked out for my baby girl." He gestures for me to approach the bed, and I'm hesitant, if only because I don't want to hurt him.

Biting my bottom lip, I move from the chair and embrace my father in a hug, feeling the tears spill quickly from the surface, the pain pouring out of me like a waterfall as I try to hold it back.

"He died protecting the family. An honorable and noble death," Dad says, as if that makes Rhys's departure any easier.

It doesn't, at least not for me.

Ashton clears his throat. "I'm going to give you guys some privacy. Nova, I'll be right outside in the hallway if you need anything."

I wait until I hear the door clasp shut and finally pull back, wiping the tears. "Ashton and I broke up," I admit. The words pain me almost as much as Rhys's passing. I climb back into the chair behind me, sniffling and stealing a tissue from the box, doing my best to dry my eyes.

"I never did like him for you. My little girl deserves better," Dad says. "Do you need me to fire him? If he did anything to hurt you—"

While I appreciate his threat, I hold up a hand to stop him.

"Ashton wants this life," I say, my hands gesturing in front of me. "It's not what I want. It's never what I wanted. Mom was murdered. My first nanny along with her. I just lost Rhys in an awful explosion with men who abducted my best friend. There's too much at stake. I'd rather lose Ashton in a break-up than any other way," I confess.

A heavy sigh falls from my father's lips. "Nova, you are one of the strongest people I know."

I glance down, wringing my hands together.

I don't feel particularly strong right now. I feel like I've hit rock bottom.

"That boy, Ashton, is wildly in love with you. I tried to keep him away; I had Dante order him to marry Harper!" Dad curses under his breath, not pleased that Ashton disobeyed a direct order. "You're going to let a little bit of fear get in the way of your happiness?"

I scoff and rub my shoes along the floor, dragging my feet. "I don't want him to end up in a bed like this, or worse," I whisper. "I cared about Rhys. I loved him like a sibling, and he was taken from me."

My breath catches in my throat, the tears surfacing all over again, and I wipe my face with the back of my hand, the tissue already soaking wet and worthless. I toss it in the nearby trash and steal another from the table.

"I don't have to ask the specifics because I know Rhys died a hero," Dad says.

Silently, I nod.

He's right.

Rhys made sure that no one survived that second explosion, that the men who have been hurting our family are dead. He sacrificed himself to ensure our family's safety.

"It was wrong of me to interfere in your relationship with Ashton. It's obvious he cares about you, he'd do anything to protect you, and no matter how much you try to run away from it, you'll always be the daughter of the mafia."

I huff under my breath. "I don't want this life. I didn't ask for it."

He sizes me up, his jaw tight. "No, but you didn't stay behind when Harper was taken. I heard you rushed out of the compound and joined the rest of the team."

"She's my best friend, my brother's wife. It had nothing to do with mafia and everything to do with family."

Dad stares at me.

"What?"

The sly smirk on his face irritates me. "You're not seeing the bigger picture, Nova."

I shrug, annoyed.

"Mafia. Family. It's one and the same."

Sighing, I lean back in the chair, placing my arms on the hard armrests that don't offer even the slightest bit of comfort.

I hate that he's right and I bite my tongue. "It still should have been a choice, my choice."

"Which part?" he asks. He adjusts the bed, bringing it down a couple of inches but still sitting up.

"Are you in pain? Do you need me to get the nurse?" I ask, noticing him adjusting the bed.

He waves a hand dismissively. "I'll be fine. I'm more concerned about you."

I don't know why he's worried about me. I'm fine. But he stares at me, his gaze heavy, filled with unease.

It makes my stomach tumble and I glance out the window into the city streets below.

"You've lost a lot in a short time, Nova. More than most. I don't want you to give up someone else because of a what-if scenario."

"It's not a what-if when he made it perfectly clear he intends to work for his father after graduation."

Why is my father defending Ashton?

"He wants to protect his family. I don't see the harm in that, but I understand that you do."

I scoot my chair back, the legs squeaking against the ugly linoleum flooring. "It's not the protecting family that is the problem. It's all the death, the violence, the threats that come with it. I don't want my children to grow up in a world without me or their father because there is always an enemy who wants us dead."

"Not every child born from mafia parents loses their mother or father. Luca—"

I cut him off before he can finish his thought. "Luca never wanted to become his father or have any involvement with the mafia. You know the only reason he's involved is because he no longer has a choice."

"He'd rather play hockey," Dad says with disdain, and he sounds so much like Dante, it makes me physically ill.

I stand, preparing to leave, ready to head back when I glance up at the television and my butt falls back into the chair. "Turn that up, will you?"

It's Harper's picture on the local news and the media cuts to a press conference about to begin. The police chief of Breckenridge walks onto the stage in front of the press to give his statement and take questions.

"As you may have heard, Harper Ricci, the nineteen-year-old college student who went missing yesterday evening has been found alive. She's at home, recovering with her family. We've taken her statement and we are now launching a joint investigation with the F.B.I. because we have reason to believe that she was being held in Nevada and their human trafficking operation originated outside of the Las Vegas area."

A plethora of questions from reporters all begins at once and he takes one question from the audience.

The woman provides her studio credentials and then says, "Can you tell us if there's any relation between the blackout outside of Vegas city limits and this abduction?"

The police chief smiles and laughs. "Those questions you'll have to ask the F.B.I., who will be offering a press conference later this afternoon with any new information that they uncover. I don't have any information regarding the blackout. That's well past my jurisdiction and pay grade," he jokes.

Dad mutes the television and glances at me. "How the hell did you cause a blackout?"

TWENTY-EIGHT

BRISTOL

I overhear Jaxson discussing with Dante that the mission is complete and everyone is heading back to the compound. Relief should flood through me, but Jaxson is tense, to say the least.

He ends the call, tilting his head up at the ceiling, grumbling rather loudly.

This is my cue to leave, but I'm a glutton for punishment. I knock on his open door and he gestures me inside.

"Anything you need from me?" I ask, hopeful that I can bail and see Liam. I've been worried about him this whole damn time. And knowing that I can't text him because his phone was likely fried in the EMP sucks a million times worse.

He laughs under his breath. “I’d love a reset, but I don’t imagine you can do that.” His stare sends a shiver down my spine, and I force a smile.

“Sorry.”

“It’s—nothing.” He waves his hand dismissively.

It’s obviously not *nothing*. An EMP took down part of the city-grid of Las Vegas. It could have been a lot worse; the entire downtown area and Las Vegas Strip could have been affected.

“Do us both a favor: don’t mention what we did here today to anyone.” Jaxson’s intense stare makes me momentarily forget to breathe. “Can you do that?”

He’s waiting for affirmation.

I offer a faint nod. “Of course.”

“I mean it, Bristol. You can discuss it with Liam because he’s aware of the situation, but that’s it. No friends at school, no one outside of the little circle who saved Harper.”

“Don’t worry. It’s not like I have a bunch of friends.”

Jaxson watches me and seems satisfied with my answer. "Where are you off to?"

"I was hoping to see Liam. Any chance you know where they're headed?"

His eyes widen and he shakes his head in dismay. "Yeah, Dante Ricci's home. I have the address, but I'm not sure I should give it to you."

I step farther into his office, tilting my head, confused. It's not like I don't know what just happened. I helped with Jaxson's involvement.

Dante should consider me an ally, if not a friend.

"Why not?" I ask.

"He's dangerous, but I suppose you're old enough to make your own decisions," he muses.

"That's right. Can you get me that address?"

Jaxson isn't thrilled with sending me to Dante's, but it's at my own insistence, not his orders, and he relents, handing over the address to me.

I rideshare my way to Dante's, because there aren't buses that go through Breckenridge, only in and out of town. Which leaves me to either walk, hitchhike, or rideshare. Asking Mom or Jaxson for a ride is not an option.

My mother would never agree to drop me off at Dante's and, well, Jaxson was already less than pleased to give me the address. Almost like it was a betrayal to the mafia boss.

Don't worry, Dante, I'm not showing up to rob you or take over your empire. I want nothing to do with your seedy business dealings.

When I arrive at the Ricci residence, there's a wrought-iron gate. It's not as though I can waltz up to the front door.

Shit.

I press the buzzer, hoping that Liam is already there so he can vouch for me and let me in.

"Can I help you?"

There's not only an intercom but also a small camera that shows who is requesting entrance.

"Hi," I say awkwardly. "I'm here to see Liam Moretti. He's my boyfriend. I'm friends with Dante's son, Luca and his wife, Harper." I name drop as quickly as I can, hoping they won't turn off the intercom and ignore me.

"What's your name?"

"Bristol Greyson," I croak and clear my throat.

There's silence for several long seconds, and I glance at the house.

Another minute passes, and finally the gate buzzes. I take it as acceptance, and I hurry inside through the metal iron gates and along the driveway up to the front door.

There are several vehicles parked in front of the house on the driveway, including one police vehicle.

The front door opens widely and Liam steps out, an eyebrow raised, glancing me over. "Hey, Firebreather," he teases and a rush of relief washes over me.

He's alive.

He's safe.

And he's here.

I hurry toward him, and the minute I reach him, his arms are out, pulling me into his embrace, lifting me off my feet and spinning me around. His lips crush mine, his breath warm and fiery as he pulls me tighter, firmer.

If I wasn't whirling in his arms, the world would be turning wildly. Somehow, the movement steadies me. Which makes no sense, but that's our relationship—control and chaos, all at once.

"I've never been so happy to see you," I whisper, my forehead pressed against his, drinking in his scent, his breath, even the smile on his face, all of it is *mine.*

"Likewise." Liam chuckles and kisses me again; this time my feet are firmly planted on the ground, but he still holds me tight against his chest, steadying me.

"Everything okay?" I ask, glancing at the police cruiser parked outside.

"As good as it's going to be. Harper is giving her written statement to the officer. They're asking quite a few questions." Liam glances back at the house, the front door shut behind him, offering us a veil of privacy.

I can't help but wonder what she's going to tell them. Will she mention the EMP or the help that Jaxson's team provided? Any mention of it could get him put behind bars. All of us are accomplices, which weighs heavily on me.

It doesn't help that I asked for Jaxson's involvement.

I'm as much to blame.

Liam reaches out, his thumb brushing against my cheek, and it glides down to my lip that is tugged between my teeth. "Everything will be fine." He pins me with his stare. "Do you trust me?"

"Always," I whisper, staring up at him.

"Good girl." His lips meet mine in another searing kiss, and I melt into his touch, his breath, his warm, strong arms wrapping around me. "What do you say we get out of here?"

"Can we go home?" I ask, stealing another kiss as my fingers intertwine on his lower back, keeping him against me. His heat, his body, having him so close right now makes me feel safe. Makes me feel like everything is finally all right.

Liam raises an eyebrow at me. "Your house or mine?"

"Your house is mine." I grin wickedly up at him. "At least until I start next semester and move into the dorms."

"Promise me you'll get a single." He leans in closer, dropping the softest and lightest of kisses over my eyes, nose, cheeks. He's taking forever to actually kiss my lips, but I don't entirely hate it.

The teasing is making my body tingle all over.

"Why? Worried we'll get interrupted at your place?" I steal a kiss from him, and he chuckles and grabs a fistful of my hair, bringing my lips back up to him.

"More concerned with everyone hearing you scream my name when you come," he whispers and covers my mouth with his.

The feel of his fingers in my hair, keeping me against him, his firm grip excites something deep within me. My heart quickens and my hand grips his forearm, steadying myself.

"You okay, Firebreather?" he asks, pulling back slightly and tilting his head, studying my features.

My cheeks flush, but it's entirely his doing. His fingers loosen their grip, his hand caressing my scalp, my neck, and I inadvertently lean into his touch.

"You like that," he says with a smile, realizing what he's doing and seemingly proud of the response. His lips lean toward my ear, his breath a mere whisper that excites me. "You're flushed, all because of me."

He's right, and as much as I'd hate to give him the satisfaction, I also don't want him to stop. "Think we can find somewhere quiet?" I ask, and he chuckles.

"No, Firebreather. Not until we get home. Making you wait is hot." He kisses my nose and opens the front door.

I'm absolutely breathless, staring at him, watching him stalk inside like we weren't just making out, and he didn't just rev up my engine.

The cool air outside isn't enough to calm me down.

Liam glances behind himself when I don't follow

and he grabs my hand, laughing as he pulls me inside the Ricci home.

My breath catches in my throat, my nerves entirely alive, and it feels like wild electricity, sparking and sizzling just beneath my fingertips, like right before you shock someone from a simple touch.

"Come on," Liam says, seemingly without a care in the world.

How does he do it? Feel so unburdened after everything that just happened?

I want to ask him about what happened, see how he's doing, but knowing there's a police officer nearby, I don't want to do anything that might interfere with Harper's story. Because I have no idea what she's telling the officer in her statement. There's no way to know how much is true and how much are kernels of the truth.

He drags me through the house; it's massive in size and I've stepped foot in some pretty fancy digs since I grew up around professional hockey players. The place reeks of royalty.

Liam pulls Luca aside while Harper is still going

over what happened. "We're heading back," he says, nodding toward me.

"We should be done soon if you want to ride back with us."

Liam glances back at me, and I nod in agreement, "Sure, that's fine."

I'm okay with waiting, as long as I'm with Liam. I wouldn't want to wander into anything sinister or untoward, but I can't imagine anything bad is happening under Dante's roof while the police interview Harper.

Luca leads us into a small library. "You guys can wait here. As soon as we're done, we'll let you know."

"Okay. Thanks," I say and peruse the titles on the shelves.

"Anything interesting?" Liam asks, coming up from behind, his arms encircling my waist, and his breath teases my neck, pushing my hair to one side.

I slink back into his embrace, the titles blurring together, making it difficult to read as he steals away my attention.

"Tell me what you did while we were away," Liam whispers into my ear, his teeth tugging the lobe.

My body instantly freezes, the tension roiling over me, and I'm not sure if he senses it, but his hold on me tightens.

"I went to Jaxson for help," I whisper, glad that I'm facing away from him right now.

His breath hovers, his lips no longer teasing me as he pulls back. When I don't spin around to face him, I hear the heat of his words at my back. "Turn around, Bristol."

I don't want to.

Facing him, knowing of my betrayal will hurt a thousand times worse, even if I did it to help him.

"Turn. Around." His voice is laced with anger, and his hold on me loosens to nothing as he pulls away from my touch.

That hurts worse than anything else.

I shut my eyes and turn around, facing him but not having to look at him. It's childish, but I don't care. I refuse to see the anger because while I know I shouldn't have gone to Jaxson, I also would do it all over again if it meant helping my friends.

"Look at me," Liam growls. His touch startles me as he caresses my cheek, his touch featherlight, gentle, not at all in tune with his voice and tone.

My eyelids flutter open, staring up into his pale blue eyes.

His lips are on mine before I realize what's happening, his fingers tangling in my long, dark locks, pulling me closer, tighter against him.

He drinks me in like it might be the last time we're together, and I pull him tighter, crushing his body against mine. My fingers tangle in the nape of his neck, playing with his golden hair, my fingernails trailing over his skin, gripping him to me.

Liam walks me backward against the bookshelf, and I gasp when I feel his hard-on poking me through his pants. His tongue is in my mouth, his breath stealing mine away, and my fingers grip his arms, my body at a moment's notice ready to betray me.

Perhaps he senses it, or maybe he feels me trembling, because he lifts me and I wrap my legs around his waist and my arms around his neck. He pins me against the stack of books, and the room swelters as his mouth moves from my lips to my neck.

Heat floods all of my senses, my hips grinding against him as my pussy flutters along with my heart.

A throaty laugh emits from the opposite side of the room. I bury my face in Liam's neck as he gently places my feet back down on the ground, leaning me against the bookshelf to steady me.

He doesn't turn around. He doesn't have to, to know that we've been caught.

Liam's twin, Sophia, caught us making out in the library.

And ever since, she's been giving me a look, a silent warning, but why?

Luca drives and Harper sits up front with him. Liam and I take the backseat, with Zeke crammed between us in his car seat.

There is a third row of seats, and Sophia is in the back behind us. She can stare at me all she wants. The only thing she's going to see is the back of my head.

Liam shifts to give his attention to both me and his sister.

"Still enjoying your first week on the job?" Liam chuckles with a wry grin, raising an eyebrow, waiting for Sophia to answer.

"I'd enjoy it better if I didn't have to walk in on my brother fucking—"

"Language!" Harper snaps from the front seat.

"Sorry," Sophia apologizes, "canoodling with one of my friends."

"Would you rather I shag a stranger?" Liam asks, laughing at the absurdity of her statement, and I shoot him a warning glance.

"You do that and you're a dead man," I say. The mere thought of him putting his hands on another woman makes my stomach turn.

Liam reaches over the car seat, and I offer him my

hand. “Believe me when I say, I can’t handle more than one woman at a time.”

I glare at Liam, unsure that it’s a worthy apology.

Luca snorts from the front seat. “Nice save.”

TWENTY-NINE

LUCA

Harper glares at me, and I swear I haven't done a damn thing wrong. It's Harper who suggested terminating the pregnancy.

Well, not in as many words, but she made it clear she wasn't certain she wanted to keep it, so I assume that's what she meant, because no one is giving away my child.

To say I'm a bit grumpy after that announcement is the understatement of the century. But I played the dutiful husband while Harper gave her statement to the Breckenridge police, who interviewed her at the compound.

But now that we're alone, well, in the car heading back to campus and away from the police and my parents, I have no trouble being pissed at her.

I get it.

The whole pregnancy thing is her body, but still, that doesn't mean I'm happy about it.

We're married.

She's *my* wife.

That's my kid in there—and I swerve back into the lane as I realize I've been drifting and not fully paying attention to the road.

Shit.

I need to be more careful because my other kid, Zeke, is in the backseat. Along with my friends.

"What's with the tension?" Liam asks, taking the attention off of him.

How nice of him to drudge up my recent drama, but it's not like he has the slightest clue. Or maybe he does? He heard about the pregnancy when I found out, while Harper was in captivity.

"Did you make out with Harper too?" Sophia jokes, and Liam tosses up his middle finger at his sister. She gives a shrug. "It's going to be fun working together."

Liam grumbles under his breath, something about this wasn't *his* idea. Can't say I'm surprised, since Liam never mentions his father or the family business.

I didn't see him ever coming to work for Dante, let alone his own father. And Sophia, that was news to me that she'd be working for my old man. But I hear it's that or return to New York and be forced into an arranged marriage.

I grip the steering wheel, my knuckles turning white.

Harper rests her hand on my thigh and gives it a squeeze. "It's been a long day, can we not fight?" she asks, her voice soft, quiet, making it so that only I can hear her.

"We're not fighting." I keep my focus on the road and shift in my seat.

Her hand falls away and moves back to her lap.

I don't want to be fighting with her, and the pregnancy discussion, if it's true, and she's having my baby, then it's a conversation we should have, just the two of us. I reach for her hand, intertwining our fingers together.

She gives my hand a squeeze; it's a simple gesture, a truce. Neither of us wants to be fighting.

And I hate thinking that I could make her feel awful, worrying about being pregnant after what that horrible *doctor* had done to her. How he violated her. I doubt he was a physician at all, probably just a perverted man who wanted absolute control.

I clench my jaw, exhaling sharply out of my nose. Heat emanates through me. The car is warm, and I turn the thermostat down several degrees. I push out a shaky breath, trying to steady myself as I focus on the road in front of me.

It's late. Growing darker by the minute. And I'm beyond tired, although I doubt I'll be able to sleep tonight. I imagine Harper won't be able to either without more nightmares plaguing us.

The silence hangs heavy between us, and Zeke breaks the tension as he wiggles in his car seat.

"Are we there yet?" Zeke asks, leaning forward, his seatbelt restraining him. "Home yet?"

"We'll be home soon," Harper says, recognizing the route. We've taken it enough times, she's familiar with the drive.

I could practically make it with my eyes shut, which at least is comforting that I don't have to stare at GPS and worry about missing the turn. I'm on autopilot driving home.

"I'm bored," Zeke proclaims rather loudly.

"Do you want to count all the different color cars we see?" Bristol asks.

I glance in my rearview mirror and Zeke nods excitedly.

Ashton, Liam, and I miss hockey practice. We text coach to tell him that all three of us came down with the stomach flu after eating bad sushi over the weekend, which seems to satisfy him when he texts back for us to feel better.

We spend the evening chilling out, playing video games, and ordering pizza for dinner. No one is up to hiking over to the dining hall to get dinner, which is fine with me. I'd rather kick my feet up and relax.

Zeke makes a massive mess of his pizza and Harper gets him cleaned up with a bath before she tucks him into bed. I kiss the little guy goodnight and grab Harper's hand as we head out of his bedroom, wanting a few minutes alone with her, before we retire for the night.

It's nowhere near bedtime for us, but we've spent most of the evening with our housemates, and I imagine if it were up to her, she'd go right back on the couch with them.

She's been avoiding me.

Maybe it's not on purpose, but it certainly feels that way.

"Can we talk?" I squeeze her hand and tug her toward our bedroom.

She emits a heavy sigh and nods. "We'll be back in a few, guys. Someone can take my turn," she says in regard to the video game.

They've already skipped her turn once, while Zeke was in the bath. Technically, I took Harper's turn as we kept rotating players in and out so that everyone can play.

She follows me into the bedroom and closes the door behind us. I can already feel the tension mounting. She drops my hand, folds her arms across her chest, and raises an eyebrow.

Her stance tells me she's pissed and I better be quick.

"Are we going to talk about the pregnancy?" I ask, gesturing at her abdomen.

Harper rolls her eyes and takes a step back, bumping into the door. "Do we really have to do this now?" She's avoiding looking at me and swipes her tongue across her lips. Her gaze is anywhere but on me.

"We have to do this sometime," I say. "And we should have an actual doctor examine you."

"No!" Harper's eyes widen and she finally meets my stare.

"After what you went through—"

She cuts me off. "Precisely! I'm not ready for that,

Luca. I need time." She pushes past me and paces the length of our bedroom. "No one is touching me!"

"Okay." I run a hand through my hair and take a step back, leaning against the dresser. "It would be good for you to talk to someone about what happened."

Her dark laughs startles me.

"You want me to tell a therapist how I work for the mafia?" She stares at me seriously, not the least bit amused by my suggestion.

"I'm sure my father has a therapist available who is well-aware of his business dealings and knows not only how to be discreet, but keep confidentiality."

"I'm not talking to a therapist. I'm not crazy!" Harper glares at me.

I hold up my hands in surrender. "I never called you crazy. You were kidnapped, Harper. Talking to someone, anyone, it would probably be a good idea. It might even help."

She adverts her gaze, avoiding my stare and stops pacing. "I'm not broken." Her words are barely audible, hardly above a whisper.

They break my heart.

"I promise, I never thought you were," I say. Slowly, I reach out for her, wanting her to tell me if she doesn't want me to touch her, but those words never come.

She falls into my embrace, her body melding with mine as I envelop her in a hug. "You are the strongest person I know," I whisper, my hands firm on her back, and I mean every word. Not everyone could endure what she went through and come out tougher.

Harper pulls back slightly, her glassy eyes staring up at me. "You hate me for not wanting this pregnancy."

Exhaling, I pull her closer, tighter. "I could never hate you."

Her face grazes my neck, her tears silent but moistening my skin as I hold her in my arms. My heart shatters for what she went through because of *them*. Those monsters, the DeLucas.

I'd murder all of them if they weren't already dead, if we hadn't already destroyed their organization and home. That's the only light I see right now, that and Harper, she's alive. She's home, with me.

I'd blame my father, but I'm as much responsible as he is. And while I'm certain Livia and her posse are dead, who is to say someone else won't rise up and claim her throne?

"I'll talk to my father in the morning," I whisper.

Slowly, she pulls back, wipes the stray tears with the back of her hand and sniffles, glancing up at me.

Seeing the tears breaks my heart all over again.

I'd kill to protect my wife and my family.

"What?" she asks, her brow furrowing with concern. "We just spent the past hour with him. Did you forget to tell him something?"

My fingers graze her cheek, and then I push a strand of her blonde tresses behind her ear as she leans into my touch. "Yes, that you're no longer going to be working for him."

Harper remains silent, staring at me, perhaps wondering what that means.

"You'll work for me."

She pulls back, her brow pinches, and takes a

physical step away from me, like I hit a nerve. "I thought we were equals."

"We are, that isn't how I meant it."

"That's what you said. I'll work for you," she says, repeating my own words, and I grimace. She folds her arms across her chest, tilting her head slightly as she glares at me.

"You shouldn't have to shoulder the responsibility of working for my father or being part of the mafia. You've done enough."

Slowly, I reach for Harper, my hands grazing her arms, untangling her hold around herself as I pull her to me. Her body is slack, she's not entirely fighting me, but she's not ready to embrace me yet, either.

I guide my thumb to her chin, tilting her head up slightly, forcing her to look at me. "This isn't your fight."

"But it is," she says, glaring at me. "Why can't you see that if you're involved, so am I? I don't want to be your mother, on the sidelines, not involved in Dante's business dealings."

Smirking, I nuzzle her nose, my breath teasing her as I kiss her cheek. "Babe, my mom knows everything that goes on with the business. She might pretend not to know, but they share everything. She even offers input, the guys just don't see her as one of them."

"Precisely!" Her eyes light up. "I should be equal, it's *our* enterprise."

Harper pulls back and I tighten my hold, keeping her hips pressed against mine. I refuse to let her go, *ever*. She's mine.

"Technically, the business belongs to my father," I remind her. Dante runs the mafia, he's not handing over the reins just yet. One day, he will, either when he dies or retires. I'm not sure which it'll be, but given the amount of violence, death seems more likely.

"I'm not working for you." Harper stares me dead in the eyes, her jaw tightens.

"Fine," I say and smirk, laughing under my breath. "I'd have convinced him to let you go, not force you to work for the family at all, but I get the feeling that won't make you happy either."

"We're a team. A partnership. If you're involved, then so am I." She's filled with tenacity and there's a fire behind her dark gaze. "We do this together, Luca."

My jaw ticks. I had fully intended to tell my father that Harper is out. I was ready to give up my dream of playing professional hockey to protect my wife.

Leaning in, I kiss her and then pull away, glancing at the floor, my mind a million other places right now. I had it all figured out. I'd go on to run the family business. Harper would take care of Zeke, finish college, graduate, and get a job outside the business.

She'd be safe—safer than working alongside the mafia, at least. But so long as I work for Dante, there will always be threats. Threats to my wife, my son, the family.

Even with the DeLucas dead, there are always rivals, new and old. You don't run an organization without creating a few enemies along the way.

I pull back, stalking toward the door.

"Luca?" Harper's voice is soft and warm, like honey, filled with concern. "Love, where are you going?"

"I don't want anything to happen to you."

THIRTY

HARPER

Luca is so damn broody. From the moment I admitted I wasn't sure I wanted to keep the baby, to him telling me that he'd let me out of my obligations to the mafia, he's been like a dark storm cloud. Worse, his mood seems to be contagious around here.

Liam and Ashton have been no better. Ashton has been moping around even more since his breakup with Nova. I swear they'll figure it out and get back together, but it hasn't happened yet. Liam, on the other hand, he's been even more protective of Sophia, now that she's working for Dante. Questioning where she's going, what she's doing. It's unnerving for her and annoying as hell for me to listen to daily.

Dare I admit I'm worried about Luca, but telling him that, it'll only make him more focused on *me*.

That's not what I want.

Zeke is at preschool during the afternoon, which makes studying between classes easier. My mind has been a haze since the abduction. Whenever I'm outside, I find myself glancing over my shoulder, taking note of the people around me.

I've been carrying mace on my keychain and a small Swiss Army knife in my backpack, a sort of *just in case*.

Livia DeLuca is dead.

I shouldn't have to fear a dead woman. The entire organization died with her in that second explosion, when Rhys sacrificed himself.

He was named on the news as a war hero who police believe witnessed Harper's abduction and took it upon himself to save her.

At least that's the story that was spun, making it so that Rhys didn't die in vain.

Doesn't mask the pain that he's still dead.

I've seen the grief in Nova's gaze, the tears she tries to hide. At least Ashton has been there to comfort her.

"How's the studying going?" Ashton saunters by me, glancing at my books.

"I have to write a paper, and I can't get more than a few sentences out before deleting all of it and starting over."

"Sounds frustrating."

I huff under my breath. "Understatement of the century."

That gets a smile out of him.

"What are you up to?" I glance up at him; it's not like him to be home already from classes. Or he's usually spending every waking hour with Nova. Those two were practically like Velcro before the breakup.

He bites down on an apple and sighs, grabbing the chair at the table, turning it around to sit backward on it as he faces me. "I need your help."

"That depends," I say, unsure what he wants *help*

with and if I'm willing to do it. It's not like I don't have a lot going on as it is, but I'm willing to listen.

Ashton nods. "Fair enough. I need your help in winning back Nova."

I open my mouth and shut it. "I don't know, Ashton."

He stares at me, silently pleading for help. I swear he's giving me the sad puppy dog eyes and pouty lip.

"Please, Harper. You know how much I care about her."

I'm skeptical. Meddling in other people's relationships doesn't seem like a wise decision. Nova and I are friends. I don't want to overstep that boundary.

"Please," he pleads with me again.

"Listen, I love you and I love Nova. But you guys have to work it out together. I can't be interfering in your relationship."

Ashton leans his head back and rubs his eyes. "It's not a relationship if we're not together."

"But you were," I say and point at him. "You have to do this on your own."

"Come on. How about we go on a double date? You and Luca. Nova and me?" Ashton asks, waiting for my answer.

"And who is going to watch Zeke?"

Ashton laughs, hanging his head, clearly having forgotten about my little guy.

"How about you come up with some grand romantic gesture, and I'll convince Nova to show up at the right time and place?"

Slowly, he nods, glancing at me. "Not a bad plan. Any suggestions?"

I decided not to ask Ashton what he planned on doing with Nova. I didn't want to accidentally spoil the surprise.

The three of us, Nova, Zeke, and I, saunter through the mall for the afternoon. I have less than an hour until I drop Nova off with Ashton nearby.

"Mama, candy store!" Zeke squeals, pointing excitedly at the bright and colorful display of sweets in the window. He tugs my hand and drags me running right toward the shop. I scoop him up in my arms, careful to make sure that he doesn't shove his hands into the bins as we step inside.

The place smells like cotton candy and bubble gum.

"I'm going to wait outside," Nova says, ruffling Zeke's hair before heading toward a bench.

Carrying Zeke on my hip, I head inside the candy shop and round the corner, laughing when I see who I've run into. "Hey, stranger."

THIRTY-ONE

NOVA

Glancing up from my phone, Harper and Zeke have been taking a while in the candy store. I was tempted to go inside, but I also knew that if I did, there was zero chance I'd be leaving without spending far too much money, and my budget this month is already blown.

Besides, there's enough junk food in the house, not including the goodies stashed away in the pantry for Zeke. Occasionally, I steal a few sour candies when I'm craving something sweet.

Just last week, Ashton bought a bag of candy for Halloween to hand out to the trick-or-treaters, but I noticed it was already open. He's not usually the sour candy kind of guy. I've always caught him munching on chocolate, so I doubt he was the one who opened the bag.

I swear my mind is playing tricks on me, because I see Ashton walk out of the candy store and meet my gaze.

It's definitely Ashton.

He strides right up to me and smiles that boyish grin that makes my heart flutter. His dimples are positively adorable, and I swear he never smiles enough.

"What are you doing here? Stalking us?" I joke, glancing up at him.

He grabs the seat next to me on the bench. He's carrying a shopping bag from the candy store and hands me a bag of sour jellies, in all my favorite flavors. "For you."

My eyes light up and I take the clear bag filled with candies from him. "Thank you."

Ashton shrugs. "It was nothing. Harper mentioned you were waiting outside the candy shop." There's a sly smile on his face, like he's trying to hide something devilish.

"What?" I ask, the grin growing on my face. The longer he stares at me, the more my body tingles, betraying me. His stare heats my cheeks and warms my insides.

I want to lean in and kiss him, but I don't.

He's not my boyfriend.

"I told Harper to bring you to the Arboretum for lunch. It's a little chilly for a picnic, but I thought we could stroll through the gardens together after lunch."

"You hate the Arboretum," I say, my gaze narrowing. I don't remind him that it's October and my favorite blossoms aren't going to be there off season, but it'll still be a nice stroll with the leaves changing color. What is he up to?

He shifts on the bench, his body turned facing me. "Hate is a strong word."

There's a double meaning in his words, especially the way he says *hate*, but I let it go. I don't want to fight with him. At least we're still friends after the breakup.

"Strongly dislike?" I suggest, smirking at him.

"You know, Nova, I'd go anywhere for you. Do anything..."

The way he stares into my gaze, it's like his soul is looking right at me.

Wordlessly, I nod.

His hand reaches up to my cheek, his touch warm and inviting, and I lean into his palm. "I'd even give it all up. Not work for my father..."

I kiss his palm and pull back, staring up at him. "I wouldn't ask you to do that, Ashton."

"I'm offering."

And he'd hate me if I let him go through with it. Maybe not now, but eventually, he'd despise that I came between him and his family. "No."

"No?" he asks, his brow pinching. "Do you prefer me to work for Dante?"

"I'm not going to be the reason your life is turned upside down," I say. "Your father isn't going to be thrilled, nor will Dante if you up and quit. Besides, you helped find Harper. I'm grateful for what you did to rescue her."

I take his hand in mine, placing it in my lap.

"But?" he asks, waiting for me to elaborate. When I don't respond quickly enough, he brings my palm to his lips, kissing my skin.

"No, but..." Sighing, I pinch the bridge of my nose before glancing at him. "I refuse to be part of the decision on your future. What you want to do has to be up to you. It can't be because it isn't what I want."

"It is up to me, Nova, and my future will include you if you'll have me back. But first—whether you take me back or not, I have something for you."

"Besides the candy?" I say, showing him the bag and snagging another sour treat and popping it into my mouth.

"Yes, besides the candy," he says and shows me one of the bags he's holding. He retrieves a flat box and hands it to me.

Slowly, I lift the lid, revealing two concert tickets for my favorite artist. "How did you get these?" I ask, my jaw dropping. "The concert's been sold out for weeks."

"I know a guy." Ashton winks at me and taps the tickets. "Did you see where they are?"

I glance at the location of the arena and my jaw drops again, along with the box. My hands tremble with excitement. "Barcelona?" I laugh. He's absolutely mad. "Is this a joke?"

If I take the tickets, I'll need to get a job to save up for the flight, the hotel, all of it, before going. At least I have a passport, that's one criteria I've met. It's a lot to figure out, but just finding a pair of tickets had to be near impossible.

"Well, I'm hoping you'll take me, and we can go on a trip to Spain together." He shows me two airline tickets and a brochure he's printed for the hotel. "We can go as friends, but I was kind of hoping—"

My fingers bunch at his shirt, yanking him toward me as I capture his lips against mine. He tastes like chocolate and raspberries as I drink him in.

It's been too long since we last kissed.

His lips feel like home.

My body craves his touch, his warmth, his skin on mine.

I've missed him. Missed *this*.

Ashton pulls back, staring at my lips, before leaning in and stealing another kiss. "We still have our date at the Arboretum," he whispers, slowly pulling back, his mouth against my cheek and then my ear. "Unless you want to skip it?"

"An afternoon with you at the Arboretum? We are not missing it. The leaves are going to be gorgeous this time of year." I stand and grab his hand, pulling him up with me. "Come on, boyfriend."

"Gosh, I've missed you." Ashton grins and kisses me again, my world spinning wildly, happily, as I melt into him.

"I've missed you too," I whisper, leaning my forehead against his. "The concert tickets, the trip to Spain, it's all too much."

I'll have to pay him back, at least my portion of the expenses.

"Consider it an early Christmas present."

"Ashton." I glare at him playfully.

"Trust me, the concert tickets and the trip to Barcelona are cheaper than the second-hand market."

I grumble under my breath, knowing that it still cost him a fortune. "I'm not letting you get away with paying for all of it. I *will* pay you back."

Ashton steals another kiss, the corners of his lips quirking upward. "I can think of a few fun ways."

I smack his arm for even suggesting such a thing. "Jerk!"

He chuckles and wraps an arm around my waist, "I know, but you still love me."

THIRTY-TWO

LUCA

It feels good to be on the ice, like nothing else matters in the moment while I'm playing hockey. My mind is clear, my thoughts are solely on scoring and winning the game.

But every so often, I glance in the stands at Harper and Zeke. She's sitting with Nova, Kensley, Sophia, and Bristol. It's a packed house tonight in the arena.

Zeke has those ridiculously adorable headphones to block out the loud noise. He was better at keeping them on a year ago when we played.

I can only imagine the fight Harper has to deal with

when trying to keep him distracted while keeping those things affixed to his head.

Okay, maybe my mind is more on Harper than it should be right now, but I'm glad to have her support.

Ashton manages to knock the puck away from the Tigers and shoots it to me just as the rival team comes closing in.

I'm still ahead, by only a few seconds, but it's enough.

I shoot for the goal, but it bounces off the goalie toward Liam. He loses the puck within seconds when their right defenseman slams into him, knocking him into the boards and blocking him from going for the puck as he shoots it to his right wing to take it down the ice.

Fucking assholes.

Liam shoves Nichols off him, which only seems to incite a riot. Nichols lands an uppercut and his teammate Peters is racing to defend his buddy. All bets are off. Ashton and I are on Nichols, yanking him off Liam and Peters yanks Ashton backward.

I swear the referees enjoy the show a little too long before they finally intervene.

Nichols gets sent to the penalty box right before the second period is over. The score is an even match, with no one having put any pucks into the goal.

Coach harps on us to do better when we're in the locker room during intermission.

"I've seen you play better," he grunts at us.

If it's supposed to be an inspiring speech, it's clearly lacking. The assistant coach whispers something into his ear and any light in his eyes vanishes when he stares at me. The bottom of my stomach drops, based solely on the ghastly expression.

"Luca, a word," coach says, and between his tone and the fact he's calling me out by my first name, it's like spiders crawling along my spine.

The rest of the team heads out of the locker room for the ice. Ashton glances back at me. I nod for him to go.

"What is it?" I ask. "Is it Harper? Zeke?"

Coach rests his hands on my shoulders. "Take a minute to breathe. It's probably nothing, just precautionary, but your wife is being taken to the hospital right now."

"Since when is going to the hospital precautionary?" I pull out of his grasp and start stripping out of my gear. If he's expecting me to play right now, he's sorely mistaken.

"Go be with your wife," Coach says and pats me on the back before he heads out with the team.

My helmet, skates, that sort of stuff, I leave beside my locker. I chance a glance out into the hallway. Thankfully, Bristol, Kensley, and Sophia are waiting.

"What the hell's going on?"

"Daddy!" Zeke says and reaches for me out of Bristol's arms.

I take him and he makes a face. "You stink."

"I need to shower," I grumble, turning my attention to the girls, waiting for them to inform me on what is going on with Harper.

"She's bleeding," Bristol says, her voice soft, tentative, almost like she's afraid to break the news.

"What? Where? How'd she get hurt?" I race with the questions, needing to know what we're dealing with. Did some asshole in the stands pick a fight with her? I hadn't seen anything happen, but I'd been in the locker room, what had I missed?

"She's pregnant," Sophia voices.

It hits me like getting the wind knocked out of me on the ice. I hand Zeke back to the girls, and he chooses Bristol to climb into her arms.

"I've got to shower real fast and get out of my jersey. Give me five minutes." I don't wait to hear their response as I hightail my ass back into the locker room.

I'm done with my shower in three minutes, the water chilly when I jump in, but I don't care. I don't wait for it to warm before I soap up my body and wash my hair. I towel dry and dress, slipping on my tennis shoes as I'm walking out of the locker room a second time in a matter of minutes.

There's only one hospital near the university. I don't have to ask any of the girls where Harper was taken.

Bristol and Sophia offer to watch Zeke for me. I'm not even sure if they'll let me bring him into the emergency room with me.

It feels like forever with the uncertainty and worry. I jog back to the house to pick up my car. At least we played at home tonight. Guilt ebbs at me for abandoning the team, but my wife, Harper, she always comes first.

I park outside the emergency room in the visitor lot and hurry in through the double doors, demanding to know where they took my wife. There's a lot of confusion and being told to sit and wait for someone, which doesn't help my fraught nerves.

"No!" I demand, needing to see her. "Was she brought in yet? She was coming via ambulance."

"The hospital doesn't have her name yet, but she could still be in the back being admitted," the woman at the front desk says.

"I'm her husband. Can't you go look?"

They don't buzz me back and the doors have security locks, so I can't just walk in against orders, because if I could, I'd already be in the back with Harper.

"I'm sorry, sir, but you're going to have to take a seat in our waiting area. As soon as we have more information, we'll let you know."

"Please, she's pregnant," I say, pleading with the woman at the desk. "Can't you get up and check to see if she's here? Please. I'm sure she's frightened and scared to be alone."

An officer stalks up to the desk. "Everything all right here?" he asks, glancing me over.

Is it that obvious I'm frazzled? The last thing I want is to get kicked out of this place.

The security door unlocks, and it slowly opens. If the officer wasn't sizing me up, I'd consider making a dash for it, but if I get arrested, it'll be even longer until I see Harper.

"Luca!" Nova's voice carries through the hall as she comes out from the emergency room. "Harper's being seen right now. Come on," Nova says and gestures for me to come through the door.

"Thanks for all your help," I snarl sarcastically at the receptionist as I hurry for the door.

Nova hits the button, making sure it stays open extra-long while I head back and have half a mind to toss my middle finger up at the officer for taking *her* side.

"Thanks," I say, grateful Nova went with Harper to the hospital. "What's going on?"

She walks at a fast clip and I'm right alongside of her, keeping up with her strides. "She's just down this hallway," Nova says. "She started having cramping and bleeding."

My breath catches and I nod weakly. "The baby?"

"I don't know yet." Nova leads me through the maze of hallways and to the room where Harper is being kept. She pulls back the curtain. "Look who I found."

Harper's cheeks are red, her face splotchy from crying, and the moment she latches onto my hand and meets my stare, her dark eyes begin to water.

It makes my chest ache.

"Hey, I'm right here," I say, offering a forced smile, trying to cheer her up. "How are you feeling?"

"The pain is better. But there was blood." She glances away, biting her bottom lip to keep the tears from falling. "Where's Zeke?" Harper sniffles, and Nova hands her a tissue.

"He's at home with Sophia and Bristol. They're playing babysitter tonight." I squeeze her hand. "He's fine. Have you seen the doctor yet?"

"Just the nurse," Nova says.

Within half an hour, the doctor comes in, examines Harper, and orders a plethora of tests, including an ultrasound, bloodwork, among other things that I'm unfamiliar with. Nova grabs me a chair so that I can sit with Harper while she takes the accompanying chair. There's not a lot of space in the emergency room, but I'm just glad to be with her.

Nova's phone buzzes and she glances at the text. I imagine it's Ashton, asking what happened.

"Did you guys win the game?" Harper asks after the doctor leaves and we're waiting for the tech to come in and perform an ultrasound.

"Don't know, I left as soon as I heard you were taken to the hospital."

"You left the game?" Harper moves to sit up, and I

gently touch her shoulder, gesturing for her to stay put.

"You're more important to me than hockey."

After the tests, exams, and listening to our baby's heartbeat, we're informed that everything is fine with the baby. The doctor explains in thorough detail the reason for her bleeding, but my brain is a million miles away.

Our baby is healthy.

I inhale sharply, feel the first sting of tears, and swallow it back down before they have time to surface.

Harper emits a quiet sob, and I offer her a hug, my hands gently grazing over her shoulder, trying to reassure her that she's okay.

As soon as the doctor leaves, she wipes the tears away.

I can't read her expression, as the overwhelming emotions pour out of her. "I thought I lost it," she whispers, rubbing at the tears, swiping them away as they fall faster down her cheek.

Nova offers another tissue, and I'm right at Harper's side, silent, listening, doing what I can to offer comfort.

"I didn't know how much I wanted this baby," she rests a hand on her abdomen, "until I thought I lost it."

I inhale sharply, the air sucked out of my lungs.

Is she saying what I think she's saying?

"You want to keep the baby?" I ask, trying not to get my hopes up for fear that she'll shatter my heart.

Harper wordlessly nods. More tears fall, and I lean down, hugging and kissing her. "Babe, I want that too. But are you sure?"

"As sure as I am about us managing two kids." She laughs between tears.

I grab a tissue and dab at her eyes, trying to make her feel better. "I promise we'll figure it out together."

There's been silence from the DeLucas. My father has assured me that all of them are dead. I can't help but feel like shadows follow us. I'll always be looking over my shoulder working for my father.

But leaving the mafia behind isn't an option. Not with all I've seen, all I know. When women like Harper are taken, I can't just ignore the horrors when we can do something to stop it.

Law enforcement isn't an option.

I've gotten my hands far too dirty to become one of the *good guys*.

Sitting on the couch with Zeke in my lap, there's a strong knock on the front door. It's Sunday afternoon. My father gave us the day off because he thinks we have hockey practice.

It gives me the day to spend with my family.

I place Zeke on the sofa and wander to the door, glancing through the peephole.

I never thought I'd see *him* on my front porch.

Yanking open the door, I come face-to-face with Kyler Greyson, Bristol's father.

"Mr. Greyson," I say, a stupid grin written all over my face.

Zeke jumps down from the sofa to see who is at the door.

"Luca, is my daughter here?"

"Bristol! Liam! You have company!" I shout into the void. They're cooped up in Liam's bedroom, doing who knows what—actually, I'm pretty sure I know what, and I don't think her father would approve.

"Come inside," I offer, opening the door farther and letting him enter the house.

He steps inside, glances around, taking in our living arrangements.

"Hi," Zeke says, smiling shyly up at the stranger.

"Hey, little buddy." Kyler bends down to Zeke's level and my little man glances Kyler over like he's sizing him up.

"Do you play hockey?" Zeke asks.

Our kid probably thinks *everyone* plays hockey, but he has no idea he's standing in front of a legend.

"I used to," Kyler says and taps Zeke's nose.

Zeke giggles, and Kyler stands just as Bristol comes waltzing down the hallway. Her eyes widen when she sees who the guest is.

"Dad?" Bristol glances over her shoulder toward Liam. There's a silent exchange between them before forcing a smile at her father.

Liam hasn't surfaced yet from around the hallway, but I imagine he's fixing his clothes or trying to look presentable.

"Your paperwork came through and you were accepted to Evergreen University for next semester."

"I know," Bristol says. "That's not why you're here."

"You're right. The holidays are coming, and we'd like you and your boyfriend to come spend them with us."

Bristol folds her arms across her chest and steps closer to her father while I grab Zeke and pull him to sit with me on the sofa. We should probably leave the room and give them privacy, but Harper is taking a nap, and I don't want to wake her.

"That depends, are you willing to accept that I'm dating a hockey player?"

"We're inviting both of you—"

Bristol cuts him off, "An invitation and accepting someone are two different things."

Kyler expels a breath. "I'm not happy you're dating a hockey player, but I'd like the opportunity to get to know your boyfriend. Maybe then I can make an informed decision about him."

Bristol snorts. "You sound like Mom."

His eyes crinkle.

"Is that so bad?" Kyler asks.

"I'll talk with Liam—"

Liam rounds the corner, wrapping an arm around Bristol's waist. "Yes, we'll come over for the holidays. Thank you for inviting us."

She glares up at Liam.

"What?" he asks, oblivious to the tension.

Kyler clears his throat. "I also came here to speak with Luca. Do you have somewhere we might have a little chat?"

"Yeah, sure," I say and stand, gesturing for him to join me in the study lounge. It's not exactly private with closed doors, but it's not in the living room in front of everyone, either.

I glance at Zeke and give him a kiss. "Will you stay here and watch some cartoons for Daddy?" I grab the remote and turn the channel on to something he'd much prefer, in hopes of keeping him occupied.

Zeke is hooked to the television, and I lead Kyler Greyson to the study where we have a table set up and a couple of chairs. "What can I help you with, sir?" I ask, unsure why he's asking to speak with me alone.

If he's expecting me to spy on Bristol and Liam or give him details about my friend, he's going to be sorely disappointed. Liam is like a brother to me, especially after he helped with Harper's rescue.

I owe him.

"Have a seat," he suggests as we approach the table, and I grab a seat across from him as he sits.

His tone makes me nervous.

"I've been watching your play, studying your hockey career closely. You're twenty, is that correct?"

"Yes, sir."

He's asking because the hockey draft ends when you hit twenty-one; you're no longer eligible, at which point you're eligible solely as a free agent.

"Have you thought about playing professionally?" Kyler asks.

I try not to laugh at the absurdity of the question. Of course, I've thought about it.

"What athlete hasn't thought about it?" I say, trying not to smile, hoping that he's not messing with me.

He doesn't seem like the type, but that doesn't mean since he doesn't like Liam, he might not like me.

"Let me give you my card and my information. We'd be happy to take you and your family out to dinner, answer any questions that you might have."

My breath catches in my throat. Is this seriously happening?

Is he actually asking me about joining the hockey draft? Being a top prospect is huge.

"Don't look so surprised," Kyler says. "I've seen you on the ice at Predators games and the other night when you played the Tigers. I'll admit, I was disappointed when you left early, but my daughter informed me of the reason. I do hope your wife is doing well."

"She's better," I say, expelling a heavy breath, relieved that Harper and the baby are both healthy.

"That's good to hear," Kyler says, and he genuinely seems concerned and pleased at the news. "Off the record, I do need to know if your father, Dante Ricci, will be an issue if you're drafted." His dark stare feels icy as he awaits my answer.

My jaw tightens as I stare at Kyler. My gaze flinches slightly as I can't help but wonder what Bristol told him of us. How much does he know?

The silence between us feels heavy, like a dark cloud about ready to rain down on the space between us.

Kyler clears his throat. "Emerson works for Eagle Tactical," he says, as if that clarifies his question.

When I don't say anything, merely size him up, he continues talking, as though he's trying to explain himself. Does he fear me, or is it my father he's afraid of?

"My wife knows what really happened in Vegas."

A heavy breath leaves my lips and I sigh. I suppose *he* knows as well. No one seems good at keeping secrets these days. "I hope you can use discretion," I say, not wanting it to sound like a threat but also realizing the capacity of what happened, the danger that lurks in spelling it out for anyone who might cause more harm to our family and friends.

"How do you think you flew out and back to Vegas?" Kyler asks.

I'm silent, considering his question. I had assumed Dante had owned the plane, but it's not as though we ever took any private flights anywhere. Dante wasn't one to leave home very often, his job always keeping him nearby and busy.

"We appreciate the use of your private plane," I say, the gratefulness far more formal. I can't help but wonder what he's getting at. Why tell me these things? What does he hope to achieve?

"I'm not looking for thanks, Luca. I'm just making

you aware, I know who your father is. I know what he expects of you as his only heir."

I inhale sharply and bite down on my tongue to keep from saying something regrettable.

Kyler Greyson doesn't know all of it. He doesn't know about the danger posed to my family, about Harper being forced to work for Dante after protecting Zeke and Nova when a man broke into our home to take our son.

My silence stretches on, and Kyler continues speaking, calmly, clearly, making his point heard.

"I would expect if you were drafted that you would leave the business dealings aside while you play hockey. We can't afford to lose an integral part of our team. I would also need reassurance that your alliance would be to the team. No gambling or throwing games, nothing sinister happening in order to appease Dante or any of his men."

I stare into Kyler's dark gaze. "I assure you, sir, that my loyalty, if I were drafted, would be to the team. I've never cheated and wouldn't start now. My father understands that hockey is my lifeblood. And while I might be his only heir, he has come to accept that if I'm drafted, I will choose that over him."

I leave out the part where I've promised to work for Dante after my career is over and then my wife is tied to the business. If I'm drafted, then she'll be working for my father. My stomach does little flip-flops at that thought, but there's still time to renegotiate that deal with my father.

Kyler's nostrils flare as he inhales sharply and nods. "Understand, Luca, that I don't wish to get on Dante's bad side."

I can't help but laugh. "You and me both. But you don't have to worry, I know how to handle my father. Just give me a few days to let him know, talk to him, before any press releases are made about my name entering the draft, please."

THIRTY-THREE

BRISTOL

I can't believe my father showed up at Liam's house. My blood bubbles and I'm seeing red. But it's not because he invited us to dinner for the holidays, including Liam, it's the fact he's offering my boyfriend's roommate and teammate entry into the draft.

"What's wrong?" Liam asks, tugging my hand and pulling me back into the bedroom where we were so rudely interrupted.

We'd been cuddling, half-naked, teasing each other when we'd heard Luca shouting across the house for us.

Liam shuts the bedroom door, his back to it, raising an eyebrow at me. "What's going through your head, Firebreather?"

My eyes narrow and I grab a pillow from the mattress, flinging it at him.

He snorts and dodges it, letting it fall to the floor. "You missed."

That cocky grin stares back at me as he waits for me to say something.

"Dad should be talking to you about playing for the team, getting drafted," I say. I fold my arms across my chest and plop down on the edge of the mattress, my legs dangling over the side.

"That's sweet of you, but we both know Luca is a much better hockey player than I am."

I grumble under my breath, hating that he's right. I've been to enough games to know a good player from a great player. Liam is good. He's amazing on the ice, a real team player, but Luca is the star.

Doesn't mean I like it, though, my boyfriend getting tossed over for the star player. "I still think Dad should have entered you in the draft."

Liam chuckles. “You have the cutest rose-colored glasses, Firebreather. But I’m not interested in playing hockey professionally. I told you, I’m planning on going to med school after I graduate. I want to be a doctor.”

“What type of doctor?” I press, staring up at him as he comes to stand between my thighs.

“The kind that gets to examine pretty girls like you,” he whispers into my ear. “Ever played doctor before?”

I giggle and gently push him back. “We can’t,” I say, eyes widening as I glance past him at the door. “My dad is still here.”

It’s too weird for me to do anything with him nearby, even if this is Liam’s place. I still feel a bit like a teenager, worried I’ll get caught by my father. Some habits and fears never die.

“Okay, okay,” Liam says and holds up his hands in surrender. “I’ll behave, but only because you told me to. It’s not because I’m not attracted to you.” The smile on his face lazily grows as he glances me up and down like he’s undressing me with his eyes.

"Stop it!" I laugh and shove him away, heading out of Liam's bedroom.

"Where are you going?" Liam asks from inside the bedroom as I'm already in the hallway.

"Reminding myself of the consequences of certain actions," I shoot at him over my shoulder as I plop down on the couch next to Zeke.

The perfect example of *consequences*. I love the kid, but I am not ready for one of my own. I don't know how Harper and Luca are going to deal with two of them. Hell, I don't know how Liam is going to deal with a newborn living under this roof in about eight months' time. Or is it seven?

By the time the little one is born, I'll be in the dorms. At least I won't be getting woken up in the middle of the night. I'm betting Liam will be asking to stay the night at my place for a while after the second baby is born.

Harper hasn't exactly told us the due date yet. She'd been quiet about the pregnancy, avoiding speaking of it entirely until the cramps and bleeding during the guys' hockey game.

Worry doesn't even begin to express the dread that I'd been feeling, knowing how much losing that baby would hurt them.

They're all like family, and being Liam's girlfriend has made them accept me as one of their own. Already, I have more friends here than at Great Falls, which is probably for the best because I'll be moving into the dorms soon.

Zeke climbs onto my lap and cuddles. The kid is getting big; I can't believe how much he's grown since we first met. He's enthralled with the cartoons on the television, and I quietly let him watch while Liam comes to sit next to me on the couch.

He leans in, his lips brushing against my ear. "Should I be jealous?" he teases, and I knock my elbow into his chest.

Liam chuckles and we both glance toward the hallway where Luca and my father come out, after having a rather lively discussion in the study.

"Bristol," Dad says and nods at me. "I'll see you for Thanksgiving." His stare is nothing short of demanding.

"Do you think you might have space for one more?" Liam asks.

I raise a curious brow at my boyfriend. He's already told my father that we'll both be joining him.

"My sister," he says, his voice hardly above a whisper.

My eyes widen, realizing my mistake, not inviting his twin.

Dad seems to catch on faster than I do. "Everyone is welcome. Just let us know the headcount a couple days prior, so we can make enough food."

I hand Zeke over to Liam to walk Dad outside. "I'll be right back."

I grab my coat and slip on my shoes, heading out into the brisk autumn air. The wind whips around, it's rather chilly outside.

Dad is quiet as he heads to the car. "Everything okay?" he asks, glancing at me, unlocking the door with the key fob.

"I was just a bit surprised you showed up unannounced. You could have called first."

He stops walking, right outside his car door. "I could have, but I came here as much to see Luca as to talk to you. I honestly wasn't sure if you were here, at Great Falls, or hanging out someplace on a Sunday afternoon. It's been a while since you've been home."

"You mean the new place," I say. It doesn't feel like home, at least not to me, but I know he's moving here permanently, and it is their home. They didn't just move out here for Mom's job or the team. Dad moved the team here, in part, for me. I hate knowing I'm the reason, but I also appreciate why he did it. "I'll try to visit you more often."

"We know you're busy and I'm sorry about Liam, not accepting him at first. I really do want to get to know him. We should have dinner, aside from Thanksgiving, sometime, the four of us. Five, if you want to bring his sister along. We'd be fine with that."

"Thanks, Dad."

I give him a quick hug goodbye, watch him climb into his car, and I hurry back inside the house where it's warm and toasty. Shivering, I shut the door and lock up the house, making sure we're safe.

Liam and Luca don't talk to me about what happened, about Harper's abduction, or how they managed to rescue her.

What I've heard and learned was entirely from Jaxson, which has given me a greater respect for the work Mom does, and while changing colleges wasn't entirely because Liam is here, it certainly factored into the equation. I just didn't tell anyone.

And I never will.

I snag the seat next to Liam on the sofa and Zeke climbs right back into my lap, returning to his position from just a few minutes earlier, curled up in my arms.

I love kids, and while I'm not ready to have any of my own, I'd be happy to be around Luca and Harper's two little ones.

And maybe, just maybe, I'm already considering changing my major, again. It's not like I've even started any classes yet. But seeing the difference that Jaxson made, without having to be in the field and physically risking his life, dare I admit, I'm hooked.

"You're quiet," Liam says, his fingers finding the back

of my neck, his touch featherlight as he plays with my hair.

My eyes lazily close with a smile curling on my lips.

I love when he touches me. Even just simple, light touches are relaxing.

"Just thinking about things."

Liam's breath tickles my ear as he whispers, "What kinds of things?"

I smile and my eyes lazily open. "That I might want to change majors."

"Didn't you just declare your major when you applied for EU?" Liam asks. He's curious, not prying, there's a difference in his question, his tone.

"I did, but after what happened with Harper," I glance at Liam, doing my best to keep the conversation as discreet as possible. I don't want to worry the little one seated in my lap. "I think I might actually want to work for Jaxson one day, more than just as their intern."

Liam raises an eyebrow. "Are you sure about that?"

I laugh under my breath. I've learned my lesson, jumping to conclusions. "Yes, he's a good guy."

"Oh, I know. He helped with things—" he gestures, avoiding saying certain words and phrases as well, glancing at Zeke. "I think it's a great idea. You'd make a great spy."

I snort. "I am *not* going to be a spy."

"Of course not. At least you can't tell anyone you are," Liam jokes, winking at me.

THIRTY-FOUR

HARPER

"I've got some exciting news," Luca says as he wraps his arms around me from behind.

"Hmmm?" I ask. I can't quite explain how tired I've been, maybe it's Zeke, or it could be the fact I'm expecting.

Waking up slowly from a nap, I feel just as easily that I could drift right back to sleep and wake up in the morning.

I don't remember being this tired when I was pregnant with Zeke, but a lot has happened this week. I blame it on the trauma. If I can just sleep through it, I'll be fine.

So far, there haven't been as many nightmares as I'd have expected. I had worse trouble sleeping after Santino broke into our home.

Luca's strong hand splays across my abdomen.

We still don't know whether it's a boy or girl yet. I want to wait until the birth, but I haven't discussed it with Luca yet.

There's still time.

Plenty of time until that happens.

Lucas pressed up tight against me, and I can *feel* his excitement poking me. I chuckle softly and roll over to face him. "You are excited," I murmur with a smile against my lips. My fingers slide down his hip, and he pulls me closer, tighter.

"Did you hear who stopped by?"

I shake my head against the pillow. "We had a guest? You should have woken me. Who was it?"

"Bristol's father."

The curiosity dies on my lips. "Oh." That doesn't seem nearly as exciting. I thought when he asked, it might have been my parents or his parents. I don't know much about Bristol's family, and I roll onto my back, tangling my legs with Luca's, pulling him above me. "What did he want?"

"You don't know who Bristol's father is?"

I stare up at Luca, who is smiling brightly, his eyes shining down on me, and for the first time in days, that gloominess has vanished.

"No," I whisper, staring up at him. "Am I supposed to?"

"Bristol *Greyson*," he says and stares at me, waiting for me to connect the dots.

My eyes widen, remembering a conversation I had that feels a lifetime ago about a certain Kyler Greyson. "Her father, the owner of the Ice Dragons, showed up here? Did you get his autograph?"

Luca smiles and laughs, kissing my nose and down my jaw. "As much as I would have loved to have asked him to sign something for me, that would have seemed really inappropriate."

"Why? Did he come here to yell at Bristol for staying over?" I quip.

She is supposed to be attending Great Falls, at least for a few more weeks until she transfers here.

Luca shakes his head, staring down at me, grinning. "He did invite her and Liam to Thanksgiving dinner, which may have been why he dropped by, or it might have been another reason."

He shifts slightly and puts just the right delicious amount of pressure between my thighs, that I tip my head back, arching into him.

"Are you just going to tease me?" I ask, breathy, my body warm and tingly.

His hands skim over my hips, his fingers slipping into the waistband of my bottoms, grazing my stomach, my hips, his touch featherlight and setting my body ablaze.

"He invited us to dinner."

"Oh?" My mind is in a fog. "Thanksgiving?" I rasp, trying to concentrate, yet failing miserably. Won't his parents be upset, or mine, if we go to Thanksgiving dinner with the Greysons?

I lift his shirt, and he raises his arms, letting me remove it, tossing it across the room to the floor.

His body is glorious. My fingers slide down his chest, touching his muscles.

Fuck. How did I get so lucky?

Luca merely shakes his head. "Not Thanksgiving."

Is this a guessing game?

I suck at games. His mouth latches onto my neck as that warmth flows through me like molten lava.

"Are you sure it's safe?" he asks, his hand moving across my abdomen. "I don't want to do anything that might hurt you or the baby."

I nod. "Doctor says the little peanut is healthy."

Luca pulls back slightly, staring down at me, perplexed. "You are not naming our baby Peanut."

Laughing, I lean up and kiss him. "Relax. It's just until we pick a name, but I don't want to know the sex."

"Well, that's going to make things extra complicated. Like, how are we going to buy baby clothes, and what about talking to the baby before it's born?"

I roll my eyes. "Plenty of people have babies before they know the sex."

"Yeah, well, I'm not plenty of people," Luca says and kisses me.

I melt into his kiss. How easily I could give in to whatever he wants. "No, I suppose you're not," I whisper against his mouth.

I lift my hips while his fingers deftly undress me, and he pulls back long enough to remove his pants.

"What's the big surprise?" I ask, staring up at him. "You are full of secrets." I playfully glare, waiting for him to spill the news.

"Kyler invited us out to dinner to discuss me joining the NHL draft."

My mouth drops and I'm so excited for Luca, so happy for him. "That's fantastic news!"

He nods, beaming, his mouth back on my lips, his body teasing me, his hands roaming across my breast, cupping a nipple, teasing and moving his mouth over the peak. "This is better, though," he whispers, licking, sucking my skin. "You're getting huge! I mean your breasts are growing."

I snort and shove his face farther down my body. "Jerk."

"No, that was a compliment! I meant it as a compliment," Luca says, kissing over my stomach as his lips move between my thighs, kissing my legs farther apart.

"Sure you did," I snort. I'm not angry with him, just ignoring his statement. Of course, my body is getting bigger, I'm growing a tiny human inside of me!

"Your boobs are huge. They're fantastic. My favorite new feature at the moment," he says, grinning up at me. Luca is trying desperately to get out of trouble that he's dug himself into.

Groaning, I laugh. "Oh, I bet they are."

They do look pretty great, one of the benefits of being pregnant.

I relax against the mattress, his hands and lips caress my thighs. He's beaming with excitement, and I feel every bit of that high along with him. "You're going to play professional hockey?" I ask, just as his mouth falls on my lips below. "You said yes, right?"

I don't want him putting his dreams on hold because of this baby or his father's business.

Fuck.

Does he do that on purpose to make me speechless?

He mumbles something unintelligible as he licks and teases my folds, making me forget how to speak.

My eyes shut, my fingers tangling in the bedsheets and then in his hair, wanting desperately to touch him, as I tremble against his lips. I desire to be closer, tighter, his body nestled against mine. "Luca," I moan as the first wave crashes over me, knowing this is only the beginning for tonight. We have a lifetime together, and already, I'm craving more.

EPILOGUE 1

Harper

The buzzer sounds, and Wren startles in my arms. I nurse her back to sleep, the headphones obnoxiously wide and poking into me, but I don't care. Coming to one of Luca's professional games to support him is a dream come true.

Zeke sits next to me on his Aunty Nova's lap. We're in the luxury skybox upstairs, with the Ice Dragons' other family members and friends.

"Why aren't you playing with Daddy?" Zeke asks, glancing at the seat next to Nova with Ashton. "Daddy always says how he lets you play with his stick. How it's so much bigger and better than yours."

Ashton chokes on his drink, coughing, and clears his throat.

I'm holding back my laughter, as is Nova.

"*Hockey stick,*" Ashton quickly corrects my son. "I like to play *hockey* with Luca and sometimes he lets me borrow his hockey stick because now that he plays for the NHL, I can say that I've played hockey with—you know what, never mind," Ashton grumbles, realizing that he's practically arguing with a preschooler and digging himself deeper. "Your daddy is a better player than I am. He made the big leagues. I still play for the college team."

Zeke eyes him skeptically. "You suck?"

I try not to laugh along with Nova and the others nearby who overhear him.

"Zeke, that isn't a nice thing to say," I reprimand him, but he shrugs and climbs from Nova's lap to Ashton's, as if that somehow makes up for his lack of remorse.

When I glare at Zeke, he grumbles under his breath, just like Luca.

"Sorry," Zeke apologizes, and I'm not quite sure that he means it, but Ashton ruffles his hair.

"It's okay. No offense taken."

Zeke has gotten so big, I can't believe he's only four, but I swear he'll be ready for college in a few years with the teenager attitude starting. I suppose when you live in a house full of hockey players, you pick up some of their mannerisms.

At least he's not cursing, fighting, or shoving other kids his age. And the kid loves ice hockey and skating. He's already a better skater than me on the ice.

It's embarrassing.

After the game, we wait for Luca to finish the press conference before meeting up with him. He's showered, dressed, and looking handsome as ever in his black sweater and dark denim jeans.

Wren is asleep in my arms, curled up against me, and Ashton is carrying Zeke, who is still wide awake well past his bedtime.

"Daddy!" Zeke squeals when he sees his father and climbs out of Ashton's arms.

Luca puts his duffel bag on the floor and bends down, holding his arms out for his son. "Did you have fun watching the game?"

"You did great, Daddy. You were so fast on the ice. You went zoom! Zoom!"

Luca chuckles. "Someone is going to be hard to put down to bed tonight," Luca jokes and kisses Zeke's cheek, lifting his little guy into his arms. "How are my girls?"

"I'm fine," Nova says, though she knows he's asking about Wren and me. She's being downright cheeky tonight.

Luca smiles and gives Nova a hug. "Glad to hear you're fine, too. But I was asking about my wife and daughter."

"We're good," I say, keeping my voice quiet and low as to not startle Wren. Although somehow she's learned to sleep with Zeke's outbursts and squeals.

Luca leans in, capturing my lips with a heated kiss that stirs my insides awake and tingly. Slowly, he pulls back, a wry smile crosses his face. "We won tonight," he says.

I swear, even after he's spent hours on the ice, every game they win, he's got an extra boost of energy. It's probably the adrenaline, or maybe it's the fact he scored a goal tonight that has him beaming.

"Do you want me to take Wren?" he offers as I hold our little one.

He's been a doting father, always there, always helpful. He even legally adopted Zeke, which is amazing and puts my mind at ease. If anything should happen to me, Zeke and Wren will be cared for by Luca.

"I need help getting her winter coat on," I say. It's more of a winter snow suit and Luca hands Zeke back to Ashton, who decides to wiggle right down his arms and then take Nova's hand.

Luca helps me slip the snowsuit on Wren, and he zips it up while I hold her. Our baby girl is still sound asleep by some miracle. It's also late. I still can't believe Zeke is wide awake; he'll be a terror tomorrow if he doesn't get enough sleep.

"Let me carry her for you," Luca offers.

"You've got your duffel bag to take to the car." I'm not offering to carry his heavy ass luggage.

He smirks and glances at Ashton. "His arms are free." He grabs the handle of the duffel and hands it to Ashton.

"Gee, thanks," Ashton says, but willingly obliges when I hand Wren to her father. "I'd rather carry the baby."

"I wasn't offering." Luca cuddles Wren in his arms and kisses the top of her downy head. "I haven't seen my baby girl all day. I didn't realize how much more practice I'd have to endure playing pro."

Ashton snorts. "Cry me a river. You're making the big bucks now."

Luca smirks, not denying it. "Oh, guess who I saw in the stands tonight."

"Who?" Ashton and I both ask simultaneously.

"My parents," Luca says. "Never thought in a million years I'd catch Dad at a hockey game."

"Dante hates hockey," Nova chimes and glances between the boys. "Right?"

We head outside into the cold winter air and hurry toward the parked vehicle. It's late, most of the place has already cleared out except for the players and their families.

"He could have shown up to support you," I say, not wanting to harp on Dante. He's not my favorite person, but I don't fear him or hate him. We're on pleasant terms at the moment. I've actually gained a great deal of respect for him lately.

It doesn't hurt that I'm also on an extended maternity leave, which means that I don't have to return to working for him until after graduation. It's part of the arrangement that we made when he found out I was having his grandchild.

He wanted me to be home with Wren when I'm not in class. He also offered to hire a nanny for us, but right now, we seem to be making it work.

Surprisingly, Dante showed no disappointment when I told him we were having a girl. I would have thought he wanted a boy, an heir, but he made it clear that it didn't matter to him, a boy or a girl could rule over the family business if they were strong enough. Perhaps that's what he intends for me to do after college.

"Dad has been pleasant. I think us giving him a grandchild might have triggered something inside of him," Luca says as he opens the car door and gets Wren into her car seat.

"Almost like the guy has a heart," Nova says with a laugh.

"I think it made him realize what's most important," I say. "Family."

EPILOGUE 2

Nova

Barcelona is the most beautiful city I've ever been to, though it's not like I have a full passport that I can compare it with to other foreign places.

This is the first time I've been out of the country. It's summer break and my last year of college.

The concert Ashton took me to, he even seemed to enjoy. I saw him singing along, bopping to the music. He can't pretend he wasn't enjoying himself.

I've never seen him quite so happy.

And dinner, the food in Spain is some of the best food I've ever eaten in my entire life.

The trip, the place, all of it has been absolutely magical.

Ashton's hand is in mine as we stroll through the old streets on an evening walk through town. "I could honestly live here," I muse, glancing around, taking in the sights. Everyone has been so friendly and pleasant.

He chuckles, pulling me against him, his hand around my hip. "You'd move here without me?"

"Gosh, no!" I squeal, spinning around as I stop walking, taking all of it in. It's our last night in Barcelona. The colors, the sights, the old buildings, all of it is breathtaking. I don't want to leave. One week is nowhere near enough to explore all of Spain.

Ashton kisses my cheek and pulls me along to a nearby horse-drawn carriage. I eye him skeptically and am shocked when I find out he's planned a private ride for just the two of us.

"How did I get so lucky?" I ask, climbing into the carriage.

Ashton scoots in to sit beside me, an arm around my shoulders. I turn, shifting to face him, letting my lips brush against his. "I think I'm the lucky one."

"You are, because you've got me." Ashton stretches his legs, making himself comfortable.

I smack his thigh, pushing his leg back toward him as he impedes on my space. "There's enough room for two," I chide.

Ashton snorts. "Just making sure no one else gets any ideas to join us."

Within a few minutes, we're riding through the touristy area, but all of it is quite extravagant and lovely. Ashton sits closer, his fingers tangling in my hair as he can't seem to stop touching me.

"One more year of college," he muses, staring at me.

"Two more years for me," I grumble. "Rub it in some more."

Ashton laughs and kisses me, the world disappearing around us.

Already, so much is changing. Harper and Luca have been talking about moving away from campus, but he won't do it until Harper graduates. He'd rather take the long commute than make her deal with it, especially with Zeke in preschool.

They've been looking at houses, places they can have built to be the dream home they both want.

Honestly, I don't want to imagine living without them, but I know they won't live too far away, and I can always visit.

I don't even want to think about what my senior year will be like. Most of my friends will have graduated. I'm trying to take extra classes so that maybe I can graduate early, like I did with high school.

I just haven't told Ashton yet, in case it doesn't happen.

"I have something to ask you," Ashton whispers, and I feel a soft breeze caress my skin.

The carriage comes to a halt and Ashton moves from the bench and gets down on one knee, sliding a small black velvet box from his pocket. "Nova, although we still have a journey ahead of us, I can't imagine taking it with anyone else. I want you in my life forever. You've made me realize what I missed when we weren't together. A piece of myself was missing, and with you, I'm complete. We may not agree on everything," Ashton says, and my hands tremble as I stare at him and at the engagement ring he's showing me.

"Yes!"

"I haven't asked you a question yet," Ashton says, pretending to be miffed.

I pull him up off his knee and back onto the bench, throwing my arms around him. "Then ask your damn question already," I say with a laugh.

"Always the impatient one, aren't you?" he teases. "Nova, will you do me on the honor of marrying me?"

"Let me think I about it," I joke and scrunch my nose, sticking out my tongue.

Ashton leans in, his breath against my ear. "I've got someplace you can use that tongue if you're so eager, sweetheart."

Giggling, I pull back and glance him over. "Yes, Ashton, I'd love to marry you. But—" I hold up a finger, telling him there's one thing first.

His gaze tightens, and sweat beads on his forehead, yet it's not incredibly warm or humid outside. He waits patiently for me to answer, but I sense his worry, and I drag the moment out.

"The wedding won't happen until after we both graduate. We need to focus on school, not making little babies."

He breathes a sigh of relief and raises an eyebrow at me. "Little babies? I was just asking you to marry me, not to have a litter. But you know, now that you mention it—"

I knock his shoulder with mine. "Anytime you get baby fever, you can watch Wren and Zeke."

Ashton shakes his head, laughing, his eyes shining. "No, thanks. I get enough babysitting hours in as it is. But knocking you up sounds fun." He waggles his eyebrows, and I elbow him in the ribs. "I'm all about the trying part of getting you pregnant."

"After. College," I bite out. "So help me, Ashton, if you knock me up before then, you'll be taking care of the baby while I finish school."

He strokes his chin, staring at me, perhaps imagining the scenario. "Okay, okay." He holds up his hands in mock surrender. "After we graduate, I'll put a baby in you. I think I can wait."

"You think?" I snarl playfully at him. Thankfully, I always remember to take my birth control because if it were up to Ashton, I'd be racing to keep up with Harper. "I'm telling you, Ashton, if you have baby fever, you might need to spend more time with Wren when she's fussing in the middle of the night."

Ashton groans, tipping his head back. "I value my sleep." He glares at me, realizing what a baby might actually mean. "You're right. No kids. We will be the awesome aunt and uncle who spoil the little ones." He opens the box and shows me the ring again. "So, was that a yes?"

"Of course, it's a yes!" I squeal, wiggling my ring finger at him, letting him slide the engagement band on me.

He slides the ring onto my finger and wraps an arm around my shoulders, pulling me closer. "Best vacation ever," he whispers against my head, dropping a kiss to my cheek.

"I know, so how are you going to one up it for our honeymoon?" I joke.

EPILOGUE 3

Bristol

It's funny how my number one enemy growing up has turned into my boyfriend. It wasn't something I planned. Trust me, dating Liam Moretti was the farthest thing from my mind, until we kissed.

And now, he's all I think about.

As a transfer student, I've settled into Evergreen University. I live in the dorms, and I have a single, not that you'd know that with how often Liam spends the night.

It's practically every night, at least since Wren was born.

I spent the night once at his place, and that little baby has one hell of a set of lungs on her. She was only a couple of months old at the time. I hope for Harper and Luca's sake, she's learned to sleep through the night.

Liam is always stuck in the books, as a neuroscience major, making sure to get all the pre-med prerequisites for the MCAT and medical school admission. He's got years of school still ahead for him.

For me? I've got another year and then trying to find a job. Working for Eagle Tactical seems like a pretty good gig, but Liam will be applying to medical school, and I don't even want to think about what a long-distance relationship might do to us.

But I'm sure wherever he gets accepted, I'll find work.

He'll likely be in a big city, and there will be plenty of opportunities for us. I hate thinking about leaving our friends behind, but I've already heard that Ashton will be moving to Chicago after graduation.

If he intends on taking over his father's business, he'll be leaving our small town in Montana. I don't know what Nova and Ashton have discussed about it. We still have another year of college, and in the meantime, they're in Barcelona.

Am I jealous?

Absolutely!

But I'm happy for them.

I'm also ecstatic because I heard Ashton is going to propose to Nova during the trip. I really hope she says yes!

"Look who texted me," Liam says as he sits on my bed in the dorm. He shows me his phone, and I get up from my desk chair, grabbing his device, reading the text message.

Ashton: She said yes!

"Oh my gosh!" I squeal and can't contain my excitement. "They're getting married?" While I haven't known Ashton and Nova nearly as long as Liam, I'm thrilled that they're together. I remember a short time when they were separated, and it was hell on both of them.

"That's what it sounds like." Liam pats the bed and scoots over, making room for me to sit with him. His back is pressed against the wall, a stack of books on his lap. He pushes them to the side. "You don't think it's a bit sudden? I mean, they're still in school."

"If it's what they both want," I say, and give a nonchalant shrug. "Don't worry, I'm not asking for you to propose."

Liam lets out a heavy breath of air. "Okay, good. I love you, Firebreather, but we're not there yet."

"I know, because if we were, I'd be proposing to you." I pin him with my stare and his eyes twinkle with mirth.

"Are you really going to propose to me?"

"Well, not today!" I chuck my pillow at him. "Like, in a few years, when we're old and bored with life and want to make things interesting."

Liam is bent over laughing.

"What's so funny?"

"Is that seriously your idea of why people get married? Because they're old and bored?" Liam tries to catch his breath, and he wipes the tears from his eyes. His face is red from his fit of giggles.

I glare at him and then at the brownies. "Are those what I think they are?"

He brought me a plate but had already taken a few bites from the dessert. I grab a piece and pop it into my mouth before crashing back down on the bed with him.

"There's definitely not anything but brownie mix in that batter. Maybe a little extra spit."

My nose scrunches. "Gross." I've already taken a bite, but I keep chewing it and swallow it down while making a face.

"Zeke and Harper made them."

"Oh!" My eyes widen at the realization that they're definitely not pot brownies if Zeke had anything to do with them.

Liam pulls me against him, my back pressed up against his side. "You just make me laugh."

"Umm, thanks?" I grin, tipping back, staring up at him.

"I don't know why we didn't try this when we were younger," Liam says, his hands skimming my hips, his fingers sneaking under my shirt to touch my bare skin.

I don't think he intends to tickle me, but I squirm in his grasp. "Quit that!" I laugh uncontrollably.

He lets go, holding his hands up. "Sorry, no tickling. I know the rule."

I breathe a sigh of relief, glad he respects my boundaries. He always has, at least since we became whatever this is—boyfriend and girlfriend? It feels far more intimate than a juvenile label, but we are definitely not ready for engagement territory.

Nope.

"We didn't try this when we were younger because I would have bitten your head off—"

"Quite literally." He snickers, glancing down at his cock with a wry grin.

I wipe away the tears as my own fit of giggles surface. "You're terrible!"

"Maybe it is the brownies," Liam teases me, wide-eyed, and glances at the paper plate on my desk.

I roll my eyes, knowing that he's joking. "No, it's you who makes me laugh this hard. You're the only one."

"I know something else that can get hard," Liam says with a wicked grin.

"Oh my gosh! Do you always have sex on your mind?"

He nods, not even denying it. "It's a curse, one that you can help me break."

I pretend to think about it as I climb over his hips and straddle him. "As long as the curse is the only thing I break."

"Firebreather, you're going to be the death of me."

"I might be, but not for a very long time," I whisper, covering his lips with mine, drinking him in, tasting him, my insides tingly and warm, and the fire he roars inside of me will never cease to exist.

His body, his touch, his breath, all of it lights a flame deep inside of me, and I him.

The End.

SHOP SIGNED AND EXCLUSIVE EDITIONS

THANK you so much for reading Between Control and Chaos. I hope you enjoyed the novel. Be sure to sign up for my newsletter for up-to-date new release details, sales, early release news, and more!

If you love signed paperbacks, special edition books, or discounted book bundles be sure to check out my online bookshop: https://shopwillowfox.com

ABOUT THE AUTHOR

Willow Fox has written in multiple genres. She's written everything from young adult dystopian to spicy RomCom novels. Her books have been translated into five languages and sold across the world.

Whether Willow is writing romance or sitting outside by the bonfire reading a good book, she loves the magic of the written word.

Follow her on any of her social media sites or through her newsletter!

Willow also writes kinky romance books under the pen name Allison West.

Visit her website at:

shopwillowfox.com

ALSO BY WILLOW FOX

Eagle Tactical Series

Expose: Jaxson

Stealth: Mason

Conceal: Lincoln

Covert: Jayden

Truce: Declan

Mafia Marriages

Secret Vow

Captive Vow

Savage Vow

Unwilling Vow

Ruthless Vow

Bratva Brothers

Brutal Boss

Wicked Boss

Possessive Boss

Obsessive Boss

Dangerous Boss

Bossy Single Dad Series

Billionaire Grump

Mountain Grump

Bachelor Grump

Ice Dragons Hockey Romance

Faking it with the Billionaire

Daring the Hockey Player

Arresting the Hockey Player

Crimson Ice

Between Blades and Blood

Between Ice and Oaths

Between Fire and Frost

Between Sin and Silence

Between Steel and Secrets

Between Storms and Scars

Between Control and Chaos

Want more kinky romance? I also write under the pen name Allison West.

Gem Apocalypse Series

Emerald Rebellion

Amber Voyeur

Sapphire Sacrifice

Scarlet Assassin

Crimson Crown

Royally Claimed Series

Palace Secrets

Maiden Claimed

Grave Misfortune

Academy of Littles

Little Etta

Little Gigi

Little Eliza

Reforming the Rebellious

Little Lizzie's Reform (Little Lizzie)

Little Prim and Proper (Little Kat)

Virtue and Vice

A Proper Punishment (Little Lena)

Little Brides (Little Clara)

Dowries and Deception

Delia's Debt (Little Delia)

Decoy Bride (Little Vera)

Jessie's Secret

Violet's Penance

Piper's Escape

Fiery Luna

Little Jade

Little Alice

Little Love Bundle/Western Daddies

Little Samantha

Little Lexa

Little Autumn

Little Rosie

Prefer a sweeter romance with action and adventure?
Check out these titles under the name Ruth Silver.

Aberrant Series

Love Forbidden

Secrets Forbidden

Magic Forbidden

Escape Forbidden

Refuge Forbidden

Nightblood

Royal Reaper

Stolen Art

www.ingramcontent.com/pod-product-compliance
Lightning Source LLC
LaVergne TN
LVHW100507110826
845146LV00002B/550

* 9 7 9 8 8 8 6 3 7 3 3 3 2 *